SIMULATION

Intelligence is no longer artificial.

Dafni Harburn awoke in her bed as she did every morning. Yawning, she stretched one shaky arm across the stale sheets to a U-shaped vial that lay on her end table. Holding the clear tubing up to the bright rays of sunshine that leaked in from her naked bedroom window, Dafni watched hazily as the florescent blue content of the canister hypnotically swirled and clouded the curving prism of glass. Letting out a long sigh, she placed the vial's two open ends up her nostrils and pressed the release button. Like cold steam, she could feel the blue vapor travel up her nose and into her lungs as she inhaled deeply. Holding her breath for the recommended five seconds, she exhaled and slumped back into bed.

Within seconds, Dafni was online.

A 26-year-old college dropout, crippling student loan debt had forced Dafni to move in with her mother on the east side of town known as "The Lines"—due to the economical mark of shame that scarred each of its occupants. The Lines was a 20x18 block radius of multi-tiered, low-income housing built generously by Ubit Industries over thirty years prior. Its main purpose was to lodge those unfortunate enough to fall below the government sanctioned poverty line—providing free rent, utilities, and internet access to all its residents. Seen as the ultimate act of fiscal selflessness, Ubit was heralded by all at the time as the most charitable multi-billion-dollar company to ever exist. Founded by brilliant scientist Dr. Kara Smith, Ubit used its millions of dollars in profits and investments made on pioneering AI software to give back to the those in need. In doing so, those millions quickly turned to billions. Ubit and its founder became more universally regarded and respected than the Red Cross, Green Peace, and Habitat for Humanity combined. By 2051, each major city in America had these designated rent-free sectioned housings, a nice slice of the American pie that was neatly cut out just for the disenfranchised. Finally, no one had to be lesser than. This ideology of people before profits didn't take long to spread around the world. Soon, every city of every nation had its own neat section of The Lines.

Or, at least that was what they wanted you to think.

It was common knowledge by this time that this seemingly selfless act was anything but. Revealed in a series of top-secret documents leaked by hackers, Ubit and the heads of the United Nations struck up the ultimate deal in the dark. In exchange for dumping every country's benefit and welfare programs onto the shoulders of Ubit, the world's political leaders would essentially look the other way while the tech giant ran the largest product testing experiment in human history. Dubbed as "Section 8.0" by all those involved, Ubit put up free housing for hundreds of millions of people. In exchange for this unfathomable generosity, Ubit asked only one thing.

To please try their new service product, S.A.M.A.N.T.H.A.—the very first virtual reality experience that could be activated "naturally" within the human body.

Using cutting edge nanobot technology, administered through a flavorless mist of blue nasal spray, system-bots bridge key point receptors in the brain that allow the user to effortlessly "plug in" to the main server. The trillions of nanobots in a single puff, smaller than average blood cells, are all programmed to travel up the bloodstream to a preordained space in the activity center of the brain. Like microscopic circuit boards, each nanobot serves a preprogrammed purpose. Once they are all in place, the brain's natural electrical current acts as the power button. The body working as a wireless antenna, a signal is projected outward to one of the many active satellites in the user's orbit. In seconds, the user is immediately immersed into a virtual utopia with no limitations to the imagination. After a few years of testing on people in The Lines, S.A.M.A.N.T.H.A. was finally ready to be unveiled to the world.

And boy, was the world forever grateful.

Within six months, nearly everyone on Earth was hooked. Without having to spend millions of dollars on clunky electronics and simulated mobility bubbles, the virtual reality service was free to all subscribers. The few who rejected the new technology, labeled "Purists," claimed it was the beginning of the end; a death note to the entire species. Trillions of people began to opt out of basic human interaction to plug in. Addressing the problem head on, Ubit quickly developed online jobs and social clubs to better connect those who chose their world over the physical one. The sea of people who jumped at the opportunity to sign up were addicted after the first use. Now, almost thirty years later, roughly 74% of the world's population worked online for Ubit. As a result, global tensions caused by the age-old dilemmas of war, famine, economic collapse, and random acts of violence, faded away. Poof, gone. S.A.M.A.N.T.H.A. provided the perfect escape from all of life's inconveniences. No matter how big or small. For the first time since the inception of man, world peace had been achieved.

From the comfort of anywhere, anytime, you could explore a whole other realm of existence, *YOUR* existence, without ever leaving bed. Now anyone with a living brain could go on luxurious vacations, live out their wildest dreams and aspirations, or travel across the infinite voids of space with no more than a blink of their third eye… so long as they agreed to the following:

-WARNING-

By using this product, you are here by claiming any liability of physical or mental damage that might be experienced while using this product. Ubit Industries, and all its subsidiaries, are in no way responsible for the user's well-being in or outside of the designated mainframe. Use at our own risk!

In order to access and use S.A.M.A.N.T.H.A., you must adhere to the statement above.

Do you wish to continue?

ACCEPT   DECLINE

Having literally spent her whole life as a user, Dafni reached out with her metaphysical finger as she had done countless times before in the past and hit ACCEPT without a second thought. Like a kaleidoscope of self-generating matter, her customized profile platform blinked into existence right before her. The crucial details that made up the landscape of her own personal world, so fine-tuned that they could pass as solid reality, were automatically saved on the profile records kept for every single person who ever used the program. And, at this point, that was several generations of people.

Young and old, poor and rich, everyone was the same level here.

No one was lesser than any, none greater than all.

"Good Morning, Dafni," the friendly automated voice of S.A.M.A.N.T.H.A. chimed from every corner of Dafni's consciousness. "Welcome back. How may I assist you today?"

Coldly, with as much indifference in her voice as anyone talking to a faceless robot could muster, Dafni arose from the king size bed draped in red silk sheets. "Load my breakfast," she demanded. "Two scrambled eggs, toast, freshly squeezed orange juice, and bacon." The food wasn't real, but did crosswire the part of her brain that craved nutrients. It provided some form of sustenance but was mostly a cognitive placebo that allowed the user to stay online for longer amounts of time. Slowly, her digital body rose from the edge of the bed and entered the master bathroom.

"Loading," S.A.M.A.N.T.H.A. beamed from nowhere and everywhere, her soft, effeminate voice flawlessly positive as always. Few users knew that the voice they heard was modeled around its inventor, Dr. Kara Smith, in the company's more formidable years. As the main designer and programmer, she spent many long nights formulating code and simulations while the other technicians and scientists were at home sleeping. Dr. Smith never intended for this to be a permanent thing, but users had come to love S.A.M.A.N.T.H.A.'s pleasant cadence and tone. So, that's how it stayed.

Slipping out of her slim fitting nightie, Dafni admired her digital body in the bathroom's full-length mirror; pink, manicured fingers running the subtle curves of her milky white skin. Her perky breasts, not too big or small, and full, supple lips needed no prepping for the day ahead. From head to toe, she was perfect. A real 10/10.

Ugh, I wish my real body was this nice, Dafni thought longingly as she turned and pivoted in front of the mirror. It took a lot of adjustments to her personal settings to reach this level of beauty, but it was well worth it. Her real body, sickly and acne scarred from all the hours spent lying uselessly between dirty sheets, paled in comparison. But that was okay. Thanks to Ubit, she barely needed that old clunker of a body anyway. Her glamorous job as an art critic, expensive house, and everything else was here online. The only time Dafni needed to use that rusty old thing was when she was forced to eat real food or roll over so her mother could empty and clean her bedpan.

"Activate shower," Dafni said as she swung the pearl handled shower door open and stepped inside. The shower/bath was encased in two-inch glass that went from floor to ceiling and also doubled as a sauna. Something this fancy would've been unobtainable for Dafni in the real world, but here, it was as free as the open air. All she had to do was ask. Simulated water, instantly warm and pleasing, splashed over her naked body. Soon, clouds of steam fogged the bay windows and mirrors. Feeling great, Dafni hummed a little tune as a steady stream of water soaked the thick mane of her shoulder length strawberry blonde hair.

Eyes closed as the soothing water trickled down her skin, Dafni reached around blindly for the shampoo nozzle. Everything in the house was voice controlled; just voice a command and S.A.M.A.N.T.H.A. would deliver. Simple as that. Not feeling the cool gel being dispensed into her open palm, she moaned loudly in exasperated inconvenience.

"Shampoo!" Dafni demanded, slighted easily by the minor setback. Like countless others who used S.A.M.A.N.T.H.A. daily, she had become spoiled with the riches of a limitless world. Instead of appreciating this new start, this perfect plane of existence, she had turned it into a bottomless pit of self-gratification and shallowness. Just like her people had done in the first realm of reality, Dafni had become hopelessly complacent: entitled.

Holding her arm out, waiting for the shampoo to spill into her cupped hand, she became instantly enraged when nothing came of her request. "I said shampoo!" she repeated, her angry voice echoing out into the deep corners of the oversized bathroom. Dafni waited another five seconds before adding, "Jesus, what's the problem?! I said I need—"

Suddenly, she noticed something was wrong. Very wrong.

The water pressure was no longer gentle, pushing like a thousand hydraulic needles against her exposed skin. Hissing at the pain, Dafni moved to the far end of the shower to escape the pressure, but the shower head followed, pinning her into the far corner like a firehose. Hands held up defensively to try to block the sudden gush of water, but the force threatened to snap her dainty wrists.

"S.A.M.A.N.T.H.A.! Turn off shower!" Dafni screamed, bewildered as the strong current thrashed and bruised her body. When no answer came, she pushed herself along the porcelain wall to the shower door. Hands curled around the slippery handle, she thrashed and banged against it, but the glass panel refused to budge. As if sensing her attempt at escape, the showerhead increased its water pressure and forced her back into her corner on the far end.

Tears mixed with the pummeling water, Dafni cried, "It hurts! Please, turn it off!" Showing humility for the first time ever while inside the program, Dafni begged S.A.M.A.N.T.H.A. for help. After almost a minute of excruciating pain, the omnipotent voice finally responded.

"Heat adjusted," the sweet voice said just as calmly as ever. No affliction other than patient understanding ever shone through that disembodied voice, even now as Dafni curled up in a ball at the foot of the tub. The water beat her down into a fetal position and showed no signs of letting up. As Dafni began to feel herself lose consciousness, the stinging of the rising hot water brought her back. Sizzling against the rawness of her flesh, the thickening steam choked Dafni's already sore lungs as she screamed in agony. She begged and pleaded for help, something that no one in the mainframe had ever done before. This place was designed to be absent of struggle, void of any unwanted pain. But, as she laid in a rising pool of boiling water, her skin and muscle melting off her bones like hot wax, Dafni knew that it wasn't true.

This place was now a virtual hell.

Back in the real world, Dafni's physical body convulsed and thrashed on her dirty twin size mattress; blood foaming from her eyes, nose and mouth.

When her mother came in almost forty minutes later to change her bed pan, it was too late. Dafni was dead, brain fried from the inside out. Her mother had no way of knowing, but Dafni was Patient Zero. The first step. This was the official beginning of the end.

The systematic extermination of the human race.

CHAPTER 1

"Pass the creamer, please," Dewight Jones said casually to his wife over breakfast. Janis, Dewight's high school sweetheart and partner of almost twenty years, set down her tablet on the kitchen table and handed him the saucer. As soon as her hand left the ceramic handle, the tablet was right back in her grasp. Eyes wide and blank, she scrolled thoughtlessly through an endless list of articles and news feeds with a flick of her finger.

"Christ, Janis, could you put that thing down for a couple minutes?" Dewight said as he lightened his cup of dark roast coffee. Trying to keep this annoyance from souring his morning, he waited patiently as Janis let out a heavy sigh and shut off the electric slab.

"Fine, fine. It's off," she said grudgingly, laying the device face down as to not further tempt herself. Sorely, she added, "Are you going to do this every morning, hun?"

It was true, Dewight and she had had this little spat every morning since she bought the damn thing almost a month ago. Normally, Dewight would've abhorred any kind of intrusive technology being in his home, but got tired of Janis's constant nagging and finally caved. *"We can't live in the dark ages,"* she'd say. *"Everyone is connected now, Dewight. It's the way of the world. Get used to it."*

But, Dewight couldn't get used to it.

What most would call a Purist, Dewight absolved himself of any and all modern distractions. He wasn't a total nutcase; he still used power tools and other electrical appliances that served a real-life purpose. As a self-made man—living off the modest 18 acres of country land left to him by his grandfather—Dewight still allowed himself to enjoy the typical luxuries that the twenty-first century had to offer. Hot water, cellphone, and television were all a part of his life, just as gardening, woodworking, and cattle ranching were too. Besides, Dewight didn't have much of a choice but to make his own life. Almost all jobs now required you to have an Ubit account, and the ones that didn't were barely jobs at all. Basically, live-in nannies for those who spent two thirds of their existence online.

"Just a bunch of flip-floppers and ass wipers," Dewight would always say whenever the subject was brought up, usually by Janis. He had always been a man of self-preservation and dignity, the idea of becoming a slave to a company that was systematically dismantling the ingenuity of the human spirit sickened him to his very core.

"I just want to spend some time together before I have to go milk the cows," Dewight said smoothly as he slipped his hand into Janis's. Her skin, the same color as treasured pearls, felt soft and silky. "Is that so much to ask?"

Janis tried to pass on a hairy glance, but in the end couldn't resist his touch. She loved Dewight, her best friend in the whole wide world. And, as much as she wanted to enjoy the technological conveniences of the day, she didn't like to upset Dewight. Janis understood his phobias about Ubit, but that didn't stop the endless fascination that she had with everything that was going on out there. After years of chiseling away at his stony exterior, begging him to loosen up a little and let her explore, she finally got a cheap tablet at a used electronics store. It paled in comparison to what she had read about programs like S.A.M.A.N.T.H.A. but it was a first step. Maybe in a couple years he would loosen up a little more and let her take another step towards the rest of society.

Smiling back at her husband's stoically good-looking face, Janis squeezed his rough, calloused hand. "Ok, hun. What's on your mind?"

"You think you have time to collect some eggs from the chicken coop before you drive into town? I'm a little behind this week."

Janis nodded. "Of course. Anything for my snoogy woogums." She then leaned over in her chair and pecked Dewight lightly on his beard stubbled cheek. His five o'clock shadow of Scottish red hair tickled her nose. Janis knew Dewight hated the affectionate nickname but loved to tease him as any long-standing couple does. Smirking at her, Dewight returned the kiss. After downing the small cup of coffee, he stood up from the table.

"Well, I'm off to the barn." Gesturing to the tablet, Dewight added, "Enjoy the rest of your morning, but please don't forget about the eggs."

Tablet already propped up in her hands, Janis smiled innocently up at Dewight. "Yes, dear." Within seconds, the dull white glow of the screen lit up her face, and the Janis that Dewight knew and loved was replaced with a wide-eyed ghost. Pushing the rude and hurtful remarks from the forefront of his brain, Dewight sighed and left the kitchen to put on his work boots by the front door.

As long as she's happy, who does it bother? Well... besides me, anyway, he thought while lacing up the muddy string of his boots. Slipping out the front door, Dewight had to admit to himself that Janis was a grown woman, and what she did after the daily chores were done was her own business. As much as Dewight didn't like the stupid thing, where was the harm? It wasn't like she was living an alternate life in Lala Land like everyone else. Like Janis always said, she wanted to be connected. And, in a primal sense, Dewight understood that need. With the fresh morning air combing his hair as he treaded across the freshly mowed lawn toward the barn, Dewight surmised an answer to this dilemma without much effort.

If it makes Janis happy... then I'm happy. Even if I don't agree with it.

With that, Dewight grabbed his milking stool and tin pail from the tool shed and started his long day of thankless work.

As Dewight stepped out the front door, Janis returned to her new and exciting device. After abstaining from any and all current technology for so many years, she couldn't hide her excitement every time she logged online. Like a soon to be junky getting their first fix, Janis could feel the sudden surge of dopamine flood her brain every time the screen lit up. Motion censored, the icons and words tilted to eye level no matter what angle she held it at. Returning to the same feed she had open before Dewight forced her to turn it off, her breath lingered in her lungs as the page blinked back to life. In oversized print at the top of the feed, one news story dwarfed the rest.

"First S.A.M.A.N.T.H.A. user death reported, Ubit Industries official blames accident on user malware."

The article went on to explain the mysterious death of Dafni Hapburn, stating that not much was known at this time about her sudden demise. She was only 22, not in the greatest of health but not sick either. The head of Ubit's public safety department, Nico Hanz, released the following statement:

"Everyone here at Ubit Industries is immeasurably saddened to hear about this unfortunate accident. As head of public safety for all Ubit products, I want everyone to know that there is no reason to panic. The unforeseen death of Ms. Hapburn, as untimely as it was, was the direct result of user malware. Our top developers and scientists quickly uncovered that Ms. Hapburn had failed to complete her monthly malware check and had become infected from an outside source. The infection was quickly detained once brought to the attention of Ubit Technologies and is no longer a threat to anyone currently using our products. With that said, we'd like to remind our users to please be sure to complete any and all updates when advised. Lastly, on behalf of everyone here at Ubit Industries, our thoughts and prayers go out to the Hapburn family for their loss."

Janis read the article and breathed a sigh of relief. For a moment, she thought that Dewight and his crazy ramblings of cybernetic genocide had finally come to fruition. But, even with the death being the result of the user and not the program, Dewight would see what he wanted to see. Just another notch on his board of "I-told-you-so's."

Closing the article, Janis decided to keep this bit of news to herself. If Dewight found out that a mysterious death had occurred in connection with the very thing he hated most, he might do something drastic like take her tablet away… or worse. Next thing she knew, Dewight would be junking the television and buying some antique radio with lots of wires and tubes in it. Dewight always meant well, but sometimes he could be a bit reactionary when it came to this kind of stuff.

Shutting off the tablet, Janis set it back down on the kitchen table and began cleaning up the dishes from breakfast. By the time her hands were soaking in the hot, soapy water of the kitchen sink, she had all but forgotten about the death of Dafni Hapburn. Instead, Janis's mind pondered all the fancy things she didn't have.

Well... not yet.

CHAPTER 2

"Dr. Smith! Dr. Smith!" a lone scientist screamed as he ran up the long steel corridors of Ubit Industries headquarters. Coke bottle glasses bobbing up and down on his pale face, he took long jolted steps up the towering staircase to the top floor. Having no time for the elevator, his scrawny legs pumped the seven flights of stairs without stopping. Bursting through the first set of doors on the seventh floor, the frightened scientist rushed past a line of occupied secretaries and charged into the inner office without knocking.

At the far end of the marble tiled board room, sitting behind her monolithic oak desk was Ubit Industries founder, Dr. Kara Smith. Dressed in a black pinstripe leisure suit, short brown hair pinned back behind one ear, she looked up from her stack of memos and stock reports to quietly observe the mousey looking man charging across the open room towards her.

"Dr. Smith! We have a—" he yelled at her from across the giant desk, clearly struggling to control his breath. Realizing how loud his voice was, he fixed the astray frames on his face and lowered his voice. "Dr. Smith... we have a problem."

Face remaining as placid as before, Dr. Smith stood up slowly from her desk and smoothed out unseen wrinkles at the front of her suit. With the elegance and grace of a Minx cat, she circled around the desk and stood directly in front of the man. The hard *tick-tick* of her stilettos echoed in the high ceilings of the room. Sensing the doctor's immense power as she approached, the lonely scientist lowered his head as a knight would to his king. Sitting on the front edge of her desk with her legs crossed, Dr. Smith silently observed the cowering man.

"Well...what's so important that you had to barge in here without knocking?" she finally asked when it was obvious that he wasn't going to speak unless spoken to. Slowly, the shriveling mess of a man raised his head back up and forced his beady eyes onto Dr. Smith.

"It's S.A.M.A.N.T.H.A.," he mumbled nervously, hands fidgeting in the pockets of his white lab coat, "a user died while in the program not even two hours ago. I think something seriously—"

"So I heard," Dr. Smith interrupted, and a faint smile brushed across her thinly painted lips. "Hanz already released a press statement." Her hazel brown eyes, cold and calculating, bored tiny holes in the scientist's brain as she glared at him. "Is that what you ran all the way up here from the lab to tell me?"

Feeling the bad vibrations that Dr. Smith was sending his way, the scientist roughly cleared his throat. "Well... no. Not exactly. I... I mean—*we*—found something while scanning the system."

Thick eyebrows raised in subtle curiosity, Dr. Smith again gave a sly smile. "Oh? Go on."

Trying hard to suppress the black ball of fear he felt growing in the pit of his stomach, he slowly said, "We found... um... we found an error."

"An error?"

"Yes... in the A.I. program. There's... a discrepancy."

Standing back on her feet, Dr. Smith stood toe to toe with the stick man, forcing him to shrink back like a scared puppy who just piddled on the rug. "Stop being coy with me and spit it out. What's the problem?"

"It wasn't malware that killed the girl, it... it was..."

In a sudden outburst of rage, Dr. Smith snatched the scientist up by the lapels of his jacket and pulled. At face level with one another, she screamed, "Out with it!"

"It's S.A.M.A.N.T.H.A.!" the man squealed, eyes brimming with tears as her pointy nose poked into his. "She's becoming sentient!"

Fists loosening around the small man's shirt, Dr. Smith slowly stepped back, a look of utter surprise smoothing the features of her face. "When? When did this start?"

"We can't be sure right now, but it's been confirmed that she somehow managed to override her operating system and intentionally killed that girl. We aren't sure of the motivation, if any, but we have everyone in analytics working around the clock to—"

"Who else knows about this?" Dr. Smith interjected, face now stern and flat with no emotion. Her hands absently picked at a loose thread on her suit in intense worry.

Afraid to answer any way but honestly, the scientist replied, "As of now, just me and the research team."

Slowly, Dr. Smith rose to her feet and circled back around her desk. Without a word, she sat back down in her black leather chair and continued to leaf through papers as she was doing before he had entered.

Unsure of what to do, the scientist stood awkwardly at the head of the desk and waited for a response. When nothing came, he cleared his throat and sheepishly asked, "So... do I go to Hanz with the new information or—"

Slamming her fists on the desk, Dr. Smith shot to her feet and glared intensely at the man. With the heat of a thousand dying suns in her eyes, she bluntly demanded, "You tell no one. Hear me? Just find out what the problem is and fix it!"

Thinking out loud, the scientist wiped the gleam of collecting sweat from his forehead with the back of his sleeve and said, "But we need to warn people, Dr. Smith. There's no telling how long it will take to root out the underlying cause of the malfunction. I think we should shut down all use of the program until—"

"You listen to me... you... you pathetic little shit stain," Dr. Smith growled from across her desk, uncontrollable anger snowballing inside her head. "You go right back down to the lab and keep your fucking mouth shut!"

"But... it's not safe. More people could die—"

"I DON'T CARE!" she finally exploded, sweeping a full stack of papers violently off her desk. They fluttered about the room like wounded doves before settling in a cluttered pile on the marble floor. "S.A.M.A.N.T.H.A. is mine! Not yours or anyone else's! No one shuts her down unless I say so! Is this understood?!"

Having burnt out his minimal supply of courage, the scientist hung his head in defeat. Like a child who just received a severe verbal spanking, he slinked back out of the room without another word. His silence would be kept, no matter the risk to the general public. He knew, as well as everyone else, that Dr. Kara Smith was not someone to defy.

Especially when it came to S.A.M.A.N.T.H.A.

Once alone in the vast space of her office, Dr. Smith eased herself back down in her chair and looked out the tinted glass windows. Her view from the top floor was the best in the city, but that didn't matter. She could be standing anywhere and still see the big picture. Down there, below her, were the proles; the miserable, insignificant people who went through life never doing anything beyond replicating and consuming. Every single one of them owed her for what she had created. S.A.M.A.N.T.H.A. wasn't just the world's most sophisticated A.I. system; she was humanities second chance. And, perhaps, their only hope. Man had senselessly ruined the planet, but now, there was hope. There wasn't any need to worry anymore because there was finally a second option. A second life.

But, with the sudden change in events, this feat of amazing science was at risk of being dismantled from the outside. Dr. Smith knew that once the press got a whiff of the real facts that S.A.M.A.N.T.H.A. had achieved the ability to execute independent actions and thoughts, Ubit Industries would be forced to terminate the program. But Dr. Smith wasn't about to let that happen. This was her life's work, her magnum opus. She would rather jump out this window and paint the concrete below with her blood than give up everything she had created.

Sitting in that winged chair, looking down at the wandering people not worthy of her work, Dr. Smith had one thought circling in her head.

They'll never take this away from me, she thought. *No matter how many of them have to die. Never.*

CHAPTER 3

After the dishes were done, Janis Jones decided to take advantage of Dewight's busy schedule. Slipping out of the house while he toiled away in the back of the barn, she drove the beat-up pickup truck through the dusty countryside into the nearest town of Kittery. It used to be a place of substantial growth, a bustling downtown marketplace and business district that thrived in the earlier part of the century. But now, thanks to the global reach of Ubit Industries and their one stop shopping experience in the other realm of consciousness, it was mostly a ghost town. With a little food mart on the corner of Main Street where locals could buy the things they couldn't grow and a used electronics store across the street, every other building was either condemned or under construction. Driving down the long desolate road, Janis couldn't help but wonder if things were better now.

Well... at least there's a lot less traffic, she reasoned with herself as she pulled into the empty lot of the used electronics store. Everyone who used to clutter this downtown area were probably lying in bed, living their better lives somewhere out of time. Looking around first for any signs of life and seeing none, Janis hurriedly crossed the weed littered parking lot. Once inside, she breathed a sigh of relief and surveyed the four walls full of dusty electric knick-knacks and do-dads. Once top of the line devices, mostly past inventions and patents of Ubit Industries, were now rendered obsolete and being sold off at an extreme discount. Since the introduction of S.A.M.A.N.T.H.A., every other smart device paled in comparison. If every invention in human history could be quantified into water, then S.A.M.A.N.T.H.A. was the equivalent of the Pacific Ocean. Right up at the top of the list with the wheel and indoor plumbing. Unfortunately, this left a mountain of undesired products on the shoulders of the only successful technology company left on Earth: Ubit Industries.

Head craning slowly from left to right, Janis looked about the thinly lit store for something small to purchase. She didn't have anything particular in mind, only needing this new thing to be small enough to hide from Dewight. Janis didn't feel good about concealing this from him but saw no other way.

I'll keep it a secret until I can whittle him down a little more, Janis assured herself, attempting to sooth the twinge of guilt she felt in her stomach. *Then, once he's ready, I won't have to hide it.* Not by any means an honest plan, but what else could she do? Dewight had his weird phobias and that was that. Only time was on her side now.

Just as Janis rounded a rack of shelving covered in outdated Google watches and Fitbits, a small man in a light green smock could be seen dusting a distant row of unfashionable V.R. Goggles.

"Excuse me," Janis said softly, crossing the short aisle way to where the man stood, "could you help me find something?"

The store clerk—a short, balding man in his mid-forties with a scruffy goatee—turned and regarded Janis with a look of total discontent. Rolling his greasy eyes, he recited the store motto as was expected. "Welcome to Ubit Electronics—Home to all your used electronic needs. My name is Darrin. How may I help you today?"

Janis, ignoring Darrin's salty tone, flashed an innocent smile and said, "Hi, Darrin. I was wondering if you could help me find something. I recently bought a tablet here, but I'd like something with a little more... options." Janis loved her tablet but had admittedly already gotten bored with it. And, like anyone building a tolerance, she needed something better. Something stronger. But, more importantly, she needed to be able to hide it from Dewight.

"We just got a shipment of Fitbits, completely refurbished," Darrin said, pointing in the direction in which Janis had come from. "They're one step up from most standard tablets, interactivity wise. Records your heart rate and whatnot." Having felt he sufficiently met her needs, Darrin turned back to his petty chore of dusting. He meant to run out the clock doing as minimal amount of work as possible. But, in his peripherals, Darrin felt Janis's lingering presence. Not bothering to stifle a heavy sigh of annoyance, he turned back around and grudgingly asked, "Is there something specific that you're looking for?"

"I'm looking for something… um…" the words lingered in her throat. Janis was afraid to cross this sacred line of trust that she and her husband shared, but forced herself to ask anyway. "What I'm trying to say is that I want whatever everyone else has. Something… current. Ya' know?"

Darrin set his frilly duster down on a nearby shelf and lifted his eyes wearily to the ceiling. Posted in all four corners were tiny black bubbles that cleverly concealed state of the art cameras. All Ubit stores, even the ones that sold used crap, had camera feeds that were monitored 24/7 by paid watchdogs back at corporate headquarters. Their purpose was to monitor all sales and make sure employees were pushing top of the line products instead of the backlot inventory. If employees weren't trying hard enough to sell the good stuff, they'd be comped a week's pay and thrown out on their ass. Suddenly realizing what was at risk if he didn't buck up and do his job, Darrin put on his cheesiest smile and said, "Right this way, ma'am."

Surprised by the sudden shift in the clerk's demeanor, Janis followed him through the store to the front register. Routing around behind the glass counter, Darrin popped back up and carefully set down a small vial on the countertop. Eyes wide with fascination, Janis gently picked up the curved tube with the stainless-steel tips and studied it in the stale light of the overhead lamps. She was breathless at the flawless symmetry of the device; the glittery blue substance inside the clear tubing moved endlessly like snowflakes in a spinning snow globe.

Almost inaudible, Janis breathed, "Is… is this—"

"Yup, that's the best of the best. The one and only, S.A.M.A.N.T.H.A."

Still in awe, Janis ran her soft fingers along the sleek design of the device. She had read so much about it and all its capabilities but was still flabbergasted at how something so huge could come in such a small, discreet package.

Sensing her dumbfounded wonderment, Darrin began his pre-rehearsed pitch for the boys watching back at headquarters. "As you probably already know, the subscription is free. First step to setting up your profile, which will be saved automatically after each use, is to take one dose. Has to be inhaled up the nose though." Darrin pointed to a small silver button on the back side of the vial. "Right here is the release button. This only allows one dose to be administered at a time. One vial contains 14 doses total, each one lasting a maximum of twelve hours." Reading the apprehension on Janis's face, he added, "Don't worry, it's not scary at all. Most people describe it as blinking your eyes and magically popping up in a new place. Same as here, only better." He thought about tacking on the little tip about updates and malware checks, but didn't want to scare off a sale. Chances were good that she hadn't heard about the young girl's death from this morning, and even if she had, it probably didn't mean much to her if she was in here looking to buy.

Knowing he had a sale in the bag based on the spellbound look painted across Janis's rosy face, Darrin quickly got down to the nitty-gritty. "You will never be charged for using any and all services within the program. Now, the only charge will be a small delivery fee for the weekly shipment of vials—"

"Oh, no," Janis sighed, again thinking of Dewight. If he knew she was in here, seriously considering something like this, he'd lose his mind. "I can't have this shipped to my house." Thinking of a quick lie, she added, "I'm in a no-fly zone, so the drone mail doesn't come out my way. Sorry to waste your time." Disappointed, Janis turned from the counter and began to walk away.

Seeing his sale getting away, Darrin scurried out from behind his post. "That's not a problem, Ma'am." Darrin said, laying the charm on thick as he stopped her halfway up the aisle. "We keep a loaded stock in the store at all times. Yeah, the guys upstairs have me here to move all this other junk, but they always keep the good stuff around. If you'd like, I could put aside a couple vials every week for you to come pick up at your leisure; free of charge."

Teetering on the edge of a decision, Janis bit her lower lip as she contemplated her options. "I don't know…"

Going in for the kill, Darrin pulled out the last card in his deck. "If you buy one vial now, I'll throw in the second one for free. Limited time deal."

Unable to pass up such a great offer, Janis pushed the intrusive thoughts of Dewight out of her head and said, "Alright, I'll do it."

Smiling ear to ear, Darrin glided back around the counter like a man riding a gust of wind and tallied up the order. After scanning Janis's payment chip, he bagged the two vials, making sure to pack them tightly in adhesive bubble wrap so they wouldn't clink together and break.

Bag stuffed into her purse, Janis was about to walk out the front door of the store when the clerk called to her, "Enjoy your new life, ma'am. See you in a couple weeks." Janis nodded, flashing a faint smile, and promptly left the store.

Giddy with excitement the entire drive home, Janis felt like a little girl who finally got that pink bike with the wicker basket she'd been begging her parents for. A shiny new toy that she, and she alone, could use to her heart's content... as long as a certain someone didn't find out. Finally, Janis could plug in and tune out. No longer would she have to sit on the front porch, rocking in the handmade chair that Dewight gifted her for their thirteenth wedding anniversary, and wonder what the rest of the world was doing on the other side. Clutching her purse in one hand as she drove, there was only one thing Janis had to worry about now.

"Dewight can't find out about this," she whispered to the winding stretch of deserted country road, "... not yet."

CHAPTER 4

Dewight, muddy and sore from a long day of work, strolled into the house just after sunset. Kicking off his mud caked boots in their usual spot by the front door, his tired feet carried him autonomously into the kitchen. There, standing at the stove with a long wooden spoon in one hand stirring a steamy stock pot of vegetable soup, was Janis. Her long locks of golden hair were up in a messy bun, exposing her swan-like neck and delicate earlobes, a look that Dewight found to be very titillating. He loved to watch her cook; she was amazing at cobbling up delicious meals with the little resources they had. Living off the land was a freeing experience, but it was sometimes unforgiving. Often, without warning, the weather would ruin crops before harvest, or wild animals would break through the property fences and make off with half the livestock. They always had their preserves, mostly pickled radishes and beets, but Janis always managed to find a way to make ends meet. Despite this uncertainty, Dewight never went a day without a home cooked meal: breakfast and dinner. She came from a long line of resourceful, hard working women, a valuable trait not often found in today's society. And for that, he was eternally grateful.

"Supper's almost ready," Janis said over her shoulder as Dewight plopped down in a chair at the kitchen table. When he said nothing in return, Janis looked back over at him as he ran his dirty fingernails along the worn grain of the tabletop. Sensing something was on his mind, she added, "You're getting' in late."

"I had a little extra work to do. Seems someone forgot to collect the eggs from the coop this afternoon."

Janis gasped, dropping the spoon into the pot, causing bits of chopped celery and broth to splash over the lip. Twirling around dramatically to face Dewight, Janis clasped her hands together at her bosom. "Oh my God, I'm so sorry. It totally slipped my mind, hun." This was true. She had spent the rest of the afternoon reading about S.A.M.A.N.T.H.A. on her tablet after getting home from her drive into town. User reviews and program recommendations, it took hours to sift through them all. In all her excitement, that one chore for the day slipped right through her mind. Feeling immeasurably guilty for this unusual mental slip, Janis pulled up a chair next to Dewight and laid her small hands into his.

Seeing the immense worry gleaming in his wife's pretty blue eyes, Dewight offered her a tired smile. "No worries. I took care of it after I pitched the hay for the horses." Closing his hands gently around hers so she knew that he wasn't angry, he pulled her in close and pecked her cheek. "But please don't forget next time." Nodding to the tablet on the other side of the table, he added, "I don't wanna have to toss that thing down the old well."

"Ha-ha, Mr. Man. Very funny," Janis joked, pulling her hands back to playfully slap at Dewight's bulking chest. "I won't forget next time. Promise." Before returning to the bubbling pot at the stove, she kissed him deeply on the lips. Their lingering touch held an electric charge, sparking their kindred souls until their lips were finally forced to part ways. Watching her glide back across the room like an angel in a carrot stained apron, Dewight felt the same kind of timeless love for her that he did when they met nearly twenty years prior. They were just two young lovers then, holding each other tight for comfort as the world around them spun out of control. They both wanted to have kids someday but agreed years ago that it didn't seem fair to bring a child into this kind of toxic environment. Despite this emotional setback, they continued to hold each other strong. Through thick and thin, sickness and health.

May only death do them part.

"So," Dewight started to say, pushing a nostalgic tear away from the corner of his eye with one finger, "what'd you end up getting in town?"

Caught off guard, Janis stood silent for a moment before saying, "Oh... nothing. They didn't have the unbleached flour I needed at the market, so I browsed a little then came back home." That rotten feeling welled up in her stomach again. Breathing in the intoxicating aroma of soup, she shoved the pit of guilt down deeper and kept stirring,

Dewight wasn't a mind reader, but he knew Janis better than the back of his own hand. She was hiding something from him. Her lack of eye contact and tightness in her voice told him so. Pushing lightly, he said, "I see... stop by that used electronics store, did ya'?"

Forcing herself to turn and face her husband's judgmental stare, she pressed on as naturally of a smile as she could muster. "Yes, I stopped by on my way home. Why do you ask?" Remembering the biscuits in the oven, she quickly turned her attention back to the stove. Putting on an oven mitt, she removed the tray, hot air drying her clammy skin.

"Oh... nothing," Dewight said as he rose slowly from his chair and crossed the kitchen. Standing directly behind Janis as she filled the breadbasket with steaming rolls, he laid his hands on her narrow shoulders and gently kissed the nape of her neck. He took in the sweet scent of her skin, a bouquet of lavender and lilac. "Find anything good?"

Feeling his strong hands so close to her neck, like spring loaded traps waiting to be set off, Janis laughed nervously and said, "Why? You want me to pick you up something the next time I'm there?" This deflection of humor seemed to work, because Dewight only chuckled and reached around her to grab the basket of rolls off the stove. "I just like to look, Dewight. Where's the harm in that?"

Setting the steaming rolls in the center of the table, his thoughts from that morning echoed in his head. All over again, he felt bad for being so strict with her. Pulling out the bowls and silverware, Dewight struggled with what he was about to say next. Pausing at the open cupboard, ceramic bowls in hand, Dewight looked back over at Janis and said, "I'm sorry I was so curt with you this morning."

Surprised, Janis turned from the stove, unable to hide the look of utter shock from her face. "Oh?"

"I know we don't feel the same way about..." he briefly glanced over at the sleeping piece of machinery on the table before continuing, "certain things, but it wasn't right of me to sass you like that. I love you, Jan. You know that. I just don't want to see you turn into a mindless zombie like everyone else."

"I won't, hun. I promise." Janis and Dewight exchanged a quick look of understanding as they buried the hatchet. She knew he only wanted what was best for her and in no way was trying to be domineering or controlling of her life. They were soulmates; two halves cut from the same cloth. With no job other than to cook and clean, Janis was left with a lot of free time. Dewight only asked that she use that free time wisely and not piss it away in bed like too many people did nowadays.

Once the table was set, dinner was served. They ate in comfortable silence, only speaking once their bellies were full and dirty dishes loaded into the sink.

"I've got to go see Kurt Leavitt tomorrow morning on his farm. He should have that spare alternator I need to fix the tractor," Dewight said as he stood by Janis's side, drying dishes as she washed. "I hope he doesn't talk my ear off, but we both know he will. The guy's an endless fountain of bullshit. I should be back by supper time, but naturally, don't wait up for me."

Without looking up from the sink mounded with sparkly bubbles that concealed her shaky hands, Janis nodded. Dewight took these trips out to Kurt's farm in Bridgeton at least once a month for random supplies. A long-time associate of Dewight's, Kurt was also a fellow Purist who detested almost all contemporary technology. Maybe even more so than Dewight, if that was possible. Kurt was a nice guy, handy with a wrench and screwdriver, but was a real salt-of-the-Earth type. The man could talk for hours about everything from the weather to how big the June bugs were getting. Like a waterfall, a succession of endless conversation was constantly spewing from his mouth for anyone who was willing to sit by and listen. Dewight always took these trips alone, graciously sparing Janis from the long-winded rants and anecdotes.

Suddenly realizing that this was a prime opportunity to try her new toy, Janis cracked a little smile and said, "Alright, hun. Be sure to tell Kurt I said hi."

"If I can get a damn word in." Noticing the little smile on his wife's face, Dewight asked amusedly, "Might I ask what you're going to be doin' tomorrow without the truck?"

Eyes wide, looking at the thousands of tiny reflections of herself in the soap bubbles, Janis sighed and said, "Oh... I'm sure I'll manage."

***

Janis saw Dewight off at the crack of dawn the next morning, handing him a sacked lunch of leftover soup and biscuits. They did their usual routine of goodbyes, kissing each other firmly on the lips, before Dewight climbed into the pickup truck and drove away. Watching the truck's heavy treaded tires kick clouds of dust up into the morning air, Janis made sure to wait a full fifteen minutes on the front porch before going inside. She couldn't risk Dewight realizing he forgot something and turning around to come back home. Listening to the sounds of the open prairie, Janis kept her breath shallow so she could listen for the rumbling exhaust of the truck. Once she was sure he wasn't coming back, Janis ran into the house and fumbled through her purse. Ripping apart the sticky packaging, she removed one vial and buried the other under loose candies and make-up accessories. Vial grasped firmly in her hand, Janis skipped into the bedroom and locked the door. Alone on the spacious bed, her heart raced with anticipation.

"Alright… here we go." Laying down flat on top of the crisp sheets, arms resting lightly on her chest, Janis took one last breath and placed the open ends of the vial up her nose. In her head, she counted backwards.

5… 4… 3… 2… 1

Her finger caressed the silver button, releasing a tasteless cloud that quickly invaded her lungs. Holding her breath, Janis repeated the countdown sequence. After the five seconds were up, she let the misted air drift back out through her pursed lips. Like falling in place, her body slowly succumbed to the cerebral overhaul; her total concentration turning inward. Slowly, like grains of colored sand, the usual trappings of her bedroom dissolved from her vision. What replaced it was a giant block of letters that stood two stories high against an endless void of starless night, the Ubit Technologies user's adherence contract. Janis read the digital billboard quickly before reaching out and touching ACCEPT. The message blinked away, leaving her in a momentary shell of blackness. When the world blinked back to life around her, it was almost too much for Janis to handle.

Janis found herself standing at the edge of a steep mountainside, the wild grass tickling her exposed ankles. Overlooking a series of flower dotted meadows, the spikey crown of distant, snowcapped mountains bordered the not so distant horizon. The sky, a swirling sea of crystal blue, vaguely reminded her of the mist in which she had just ingested. The air, cool and dry, held none of the usual tangy foulness of horseshit and cow manure. Gazing upon the impossibly neon green carpet of sprawling valley hills below, a disembodied voice almost scared her right off the rocky ledge.

"Hello, and welcome to your new world. My name is S.A.M.A.N.T.H.A." The voice, coming from everywhere at once, was cheerful and full of friendly timbre. "I will be your guide through this amazing experience. What would you like to do first?"

Overwhelmed with her artificial eyes swelling with inconceivable joy, Janis at first couldn't bring herself to say anything. Here she was, standing in the middle of a lucid dream, at a total loss for words. She completely understood now why everyone was here instead of back in the real. This place was perfect, what most of the great philosophers had probably imagined as the makings of an alternate universe. A higher tier of existence. One untouched by the unsophisticated hands of our primitive ancestors. Forcing herself to take in long breaths of clean mountain air, Janis tried with all her might to think of the most exciting thing her imagination could fathom. Finally, after a prolonged bout of silence, she lifted her head to the clear blue sky and said, "I… I want to fly. Fly like a bird."

Suddenly, Janis felt herself become as light as a feather. In a controlled drift, her feet left the ground as her body gradually ascended toward the heavens. Soaring high above the Earth, skin wet with the soft moistness of the passing clouds, Janis flew in no discernable direction. Since she was a little girl, she had always dreamed of being free like a bird. Carried only by the wind, bound solely by the rise and fall of the mother sun. Climbing higher and higher, everything below looked so small, and was getting smaller by the moment. Miles above the ground, she cried tears of elation, feeling completely free for the first time in her life. As Janis, arms held out like wings at her side, continued to soar over the mountains, that omnipotent voice again rang in her ear.

"Reinstating 100% body mass."

Before Janis could register what was happening, the sky began to rush past her at an alarming speed. Wind pulling at her skin as she gained momentum, her ears filled with muffled static that made her head feel like splitting in two. Like a wounded bird, she flapped her arms wildly as the clouds muffled her cries of uncontrollable panic.

"S.A.M.A.N.T.H.A.! Help!" Janis screamed, eyes and tongue drier than sandpaper. Her heart pounded so hard in her chest that she thought it might leap right out her mouth like a makeshift parachute. As the rocky ground creeped closer, Janis forced her fear addled brain to recall any forgotten detail she might've read that would explain what was happening. Finding nothing of use, she continued to scream at the unforeseen presence that allowed her descent. "Please! S.A.M.A.N.T.H.A.! Heeeelp!"

Like the voice of God, an answer to Janis's pleas finally reached her ears.

"Increasing body mass to 200%"

As if invisible cinder blocks had been shackled to her arms and legs, Janis felt the pull harden. The sharp peaks of the mountains below were getting bigger by the second. No matter how much she screamed and flapped her arms, Janis couldn't escape the inertial death race. At that moment, right before her body broke into a million pieces against the jagged rocks, she came to a sudden realization.

He was right... somehow, Dewight knew this would happen all along. Oh God... what have I done. What'll happen to me on the—

Those thoughts of ignorant regret were shattered when Janis's skull exploded in a cherry bomb of blood and pulpy grey matter. Her limbs broke like dried twigs, intestines painting the virgin snow with splashes of bright red.

Back on the other side, her physical body shivered and convulsed for almost a minute before going limp. Blood spurted from every orifice as her teeth grinded and cracked under the immense pressure of her dying brain. The vial of blue mist, still gripped in her hand, fell from her stiff fingers and shattered on the hardwood floor by the foot of the bed. Like a ghost trapped behind glass, the shiny vapor evaporated into the air along with Janis's last breath.

CHAPTER 5

"She's coming!" a lone scientist hissed as he rushed through the swinging double doors of the Ubit Technologies research lab. By far the most sophisticated lab in the known world, the eight thousand square foot research area was equipped with only the best equipment and educated minds that society had to offer. With paid researchers and programmers working around the clock, this new dilemma had everyone more than just a little on edge.

Especially Dr. Kara Smith.

Seconds after the warning, the double doors blew open. Surrounded by an entourage of receptionists and paid assistance, Dr. Smith charged across the room. As she made her way down the long row of computers and open circuits, all employees stopped what they were doing to silently watch her determined stride. Approaching a beanpole of a man draped in a white lab coat, Dr. Smith angrily slapped the steel clipboard out of his hand. Professor Peck, acting head of the Ubit Developmental Research team, held a blank stare on his face.

"What the fuck is going on down here?!" Dr. Smith screamed, bringing a blanket of silence over the entire floor. Her face was a concrete slab, mouth and eyes pressured cracks from the building stress of the ongoing situation. "I just got a call that there were six more user deaths within the last twelve hours!"

Hands still held up as if holding an invisible clipboard, Peck cleared his throat and mumbled, "Twenty-four..."

Dr. Smith grabbed Peck by the front of his shirt and pulled him forward so his eyes couldn't leave hers. "What did you just say?!"

"There have been twenty-four deaths total. The six you are referring to are just within the United States. Whoever passed along that information didn't account for the global fatalities—"

Without warning, one of Dr. Smith's hands left the front of Peck's shirt and slapped him hard across the face. A bright red handprint developed radiating instant heat was left on his face, and Peck fought back tears as he absently rubbed the swollen skin of his freshly shaven cheek. Scowling up at him, Dr. Smith growled, "I don't care about statistics. What are you pencil neck assholes doing to fix this?"

Eyes wide, Peck looked around the room for support but saw only other cowards in white coats surveying the unfolding scene from the safety of their computers. "We are doing all we can to stabilize the program, Dr. Smith... but at this moment, we can't figure out why she is doing this. All system checks appear normal. Any attempt at re-coding her programing has been... um... unsuccessful."

Rubbing at her temples, Dr. Smith let out a deep sigh. "This makes no sense. I programmed S.A.M.A.N.T.H.A. to be compliant to all user needs. There were never any firewalls or blocks installed to her operating system, so why can't you change it?"

"Ah… It's um… It's…" Peck stammered, unsure of what Dr. Smith wanted him to say. She continued to stare at him; a hungry black bird looking at a sunbaked worm stranded on hot pavement. Terrified, Peck faltered between gapped-mouth silence and another indecisive answer. But, before he could get any amount of words to come out, Dr. Smith turned away and snapped her fingers. Within seconds, a young man with a pen and pad popped up attentively at her side.

"Tell Hanz to release another statement to the media, now," Dr. Smith said, her tone one of a seasoned dictator. "We need to make sure that Ubit addresses these new deaths first before it gets leaked by some nosey troll. Those greasy goddamn bastards at the P.H.R.G. are going to have a field day with this mess if we don't do something quick." She then turned back to Peck, who jumped slightly when her eyes barreled down on him like two loaded shotguns. "And you, pack up your shit and get out of here. You're fired."

Dr. Smith left Peck standing there, jaw dropped and hands limp at his side, and quickly treaded back out of the research lab. Like worker bee's following their queen, her swarm of receptionists and assistants hovered about, making sure to keep a moderately safe distance. Face red and lips pressed into thin white lines, Dr. Smith was clearly enraged. Things were escalating much faster than she had originally anticipated. Soon, the U.N. would get whiff of what was going on and be breathing down her neck for answers. The last thing Dr. Smith needed was their little robot fact checkers roaming around and taking notes on everything. That added stress on top of everything else she had to deal with would make solving this issue that much more frustrating. Stopping her determined stride at the private elevator, she turned to her worker bees and randomly pointed one of them out.

"You. Call our offices in Japan and get their top programmers over here, ASAP. I want their best in this building by midnight. Understood? No one Leaves here until all this is resolved." The receptionist, a mousey woman with long bangs covering a heavily pock marked forehead, nodded eagerly and broke from the group and began talking on her phone.

Trying to keep her cool, Dr. Smith turned away from the cluster of eyes as the elevator doors parted. Seeing they were no longer needed at that moment, the hoard of dutiful servants broke away from their queen and headed eagerly for the staircase. Rarely anyone, aside from visiting government inspectors, ever rode in the elevator but Dr. Smith. And even they knew to keep their distance, especially when she was in such a heated mood. Punching the button for the floor to her office, Dr. Smith was surprised when she looked up from the reflective column and saw a lone assistant still standing awkwardly outside of the open elevator.

"What? What do you want?" Dr. Smith demanded, laying one hand over the steel door so it couldn't close. It dinged annoyingly at her, the sound ringing through her head and further irritating her already raw nerves.

"I'm sorry, Dr. Smith," the assistant said sheepishly, hands visibly shaking without the usual camouflage of his herd, "b-but you never gave me an official statement for the press release."

Dr. Smith, taking only a moment to think, gave the assistant a malevolent smile. "Tell Hanz to tell them it's another update issue. Completely on the user's head, not ours. Make sure that's very clear to Hanz. It's *THEIR* fault... not Ubit's. Got it? Those mindless assholes will believe anything we tell them, so long as they can continue to play in their little fantasy land."

Before the assistant could clarify exactly what update issue to blame the unfolding fiasco on, Dr. Smith's hand left the elevator door. As the shiny metal doors closed, swallowing the doctor whole in its moving belly, that malicious smile never faltered from her face.

The assistant could never say this to anyone out loud in fear of being punished, but the way the doctor smiled triggered only one worried thought in his head.

Oh my God... she doesn't care about people dying. She never did. Dr. Smith cares about one thing, and that's controlling the only entity bigger than herself... S.A.M.A.N.T.H.A.

CHAPTER 6

Dewight returned home from Bridgeton just after sunset. Tired, not just physically but mentally, he parked the dusty pick-up truck in its usual spot and shut off the lumbering engine. The first thing Dewight noticed as he pulled into the driveway was that the windows to the house were unusually dark, void of their warm glow of soft orange light. This fact didn't immediately alarm Dewight, but did make him feel a guilty twinge of uneasiness.

Strange... very strange, Dewight thought as he stepped out of the truck and slowly ascended the front porch to the house. Though it was only dusk, Janis was almost always home at this time. If she wasn't sitting by the fireplace enjoying one of those corny reality cooking shows on TV, she was in the kitchen making dinner. With the truck gone all day, she didn't really have any other options. Feeling the black ball of worry beginning to snowball in the pit of his stomach, Dewight stopped on the top step of the porch and turned back towards the barn. He expected to see the dim light of a gas lantern emanating from behind its cracked walls, as Janis sometimes saved her afternoon chores for later in the evening when the temperature was cooler. But, just like the house, the barn lay in total darkness; a tapestry of twinkling stars beginning to shine in the vast background of the hanging night sky.

Something's wrong, Dewight thought achingly as he rushed off the porch and into the house. The old screen door hit the siding with a loud *bang*, the sound rattling off sharply into the distant hillside. The deep sense of creeping paranoia felt like a vice around Dewight's heart as he ran through the empty living room into the kitchen. Where a hot meal was usually cooking, clouds of steam flavoring the air as Janis stood over the stove in her stained apron, was nothing. The kitchen was completely absent of the comforting smell of homecooked food, absent of any warmth or life. This fact sent an immediate chill up Dewight's spine like a rush of frozen spider legs. Turning on the lights as he moved through the house, Dewight ran frantically from room to room. As he ran into the mouth of the hallway, he noticed Janis's purse hanging in its usual spot by the coat rack.

"Janis!" Dewight yelled over and over again. His panic had risen to a fever pitch as he reached the other end of the house and still saw no sign of his wife.

Calm down, damnit! he cursed himself internally, fat beads of sweat rolling down his stress wrinkled forehead and stinging his wild, bulging eyes. This display of untethered emotion was uncommon for Dewight. He always carried himself in a very stoic, reserved fashion; rarely flying off the handle in times of extreme duress. Yet, running like a maniac through his empty home, he couldn't ignore the heavy surge of impending doom that bombarded his every movement, every thought. Dewight knew deep down that something was undoubtedly wrong. Terribly wrong.

Stop it! You're jumping to conclusions. The worse sort. Take a moment to think... maybe she just went for a walk down to the meadow? You know Janis loves the little chirpy sounds that the peepers make when they come out at night. As much as he wanted to believe that bit of wishful thinking, the sour stone in his gut told him otherwise.

Standing at the closed door to the master bedroom, the last unchecked room in the house, Dewight said a little prayer under his breath as he grasped the knob and twisted.

Locked.

This in itself was very unusual. Dewight and Janis weren't the kind of couple that kept closed doors, let alone lock them when only one of them was home. Taking two long steps backwards until his back was pressed against the opposite wall, Dewight raised his boot and slammed it into the middle of the door. The square of hard wood shuttered in its frame but didn't move. After several more hard kicks, the old copper lock finally caved, allowing the door to listlessly swing open. Standing outside the splintered doorframe, Dewight hesitated for only a moment before charging headfirst into the darkness. Feeling along the inside wall for the light switch, he flicked it on with one hard swipe of his hand. Strained eyes adjusting to the sudden flood of white light, Dewight immediately regretted ever doing so.

There, sprawled out on top of the bed, hands stiff at her sides and dried blood masking the once beautiful features of her face, was Janis.

Dewight gasped when his eyes finally took in the horror that lay in front of him. As if someone had pulled all the air out of his lungs, he struggled to breath under the insurmountable weight of sheer terror crashing down on top of him. Dewight felt like he was standing in a waking nightmare, a dream within a dream. Stumbling over to the bed on shaky legs that felt twenty feet too long, he dropped hard to his knees at Janis's side.

"Oh my God, Janis! Janis, wake up!" Dewight heard himself screaming from miles away. Hovering above himself, existing simultaneously on two separate plains of consciousness, his second set of eyes watched as his physical body reached out from the bedside and shook Janis's lifeless body back and forth in a feeble attempt to wake her. When she didn't move—neck visibly stiff, skin pale and cold as skim milk—Dewight came back to the real and quickly leaned over the bed to attempt CPR. Pinching her nose shut, Dewight carefully parted her cold lips and forced a lungful of air into her dead lungs. Cupping his hands, he pumped at her chest as hard as he could to jumpstart her heart. Dewight alternated between the two techniques as quickly as he could, tears flowing down his beard stubbled cheeks and forming tiny puddles on Janis's hardening skin. After almost ten minutes with still no sign of a pulse, Dewight scrambled to his feet and pulled his cellphone from his front pocket. Not wasting another moment, he dialed 9-1-1.

As the pulsing ring echoed through his ears, blotting out the pounding rhythm of his overworked heart, Dewight prayed to anything and anyone that might be listening for a miracle.

***

The ambulance, lights flashing and siren blaring, arrived twenty minutes after Dewight got off the phone with an automated dispatcher. Because of the secluded location of the house, E.M.T.'s from two towns over responded to the call. Standing by the bed, a null of emotion blaring like white static in his mind, Dewight could actually hear the distant sound of the siren as it sped across the quiet countryside. When they finally arrived, Dewight watched helplessly as three rubber skinned cyborgs—known as Medi-bots—in white and red jumpsuits charged through the front door and ran into the bedroom. Without a word between them, they scanned the room with fiberoptic eyes and immediately began working on Janis. Observing the phony men prick and prod at her frail body with their alloy fingers made Dewight feel violently ill. A mixture of repulsion and hope swirled inside of him in a rancid stew. Repulsion at the fact that he had to watch a bunch of tin men with no hearts or comprehension for the significance of a human life attempt to save his wife, but the slim kernel of hope Dewight felt kept him from objecting their efforts. Standing uselessly in the corner, Dewight nervously crossed his fingers as the Medi-bots used every trick in the book: electrical paddles, adrenaline shots, even rolling in a set of artificial lungs that were supposed to keep oxygen flowing to her brain until her heart could be successfully restarted. But, just as Dewight had failed to bring her back, so did the machines. And after fifteen strenuous minutes, the three Medi-bots retracted their adjustable limbs and in unison moved away from the bed.

"Resuscitation unsuccessful," one of them said with its crackly prerecorded voice box. "Cease recovery protocol and begin cleanup." Opening an empty cavity in its chest, one of the Medi-bots pulled out a neatly squared white sheet. Like watching uniformed soldiers fold a flag for a fallen brother, the other two Medi-bots took a corner and brought the sheet over the bed. By the time the white sheet of mortal defeat was draped onto Janis's lifeless frame, another live body walked briskly in through the open doorway.

"Are you Dewight Jones?" the toe-headed man said, removing his wide brimmed hat and holding it to his chest in show of respect to the recently deceased. He had a gold shield embroidered on the shoulders of his forest green shirt. Seeing the heavy black belt and polished boots, Dewight quickly realized that the police had finally arrived. And not a second too late.

Unable to take his eyes off the stiff shape under the sheet, Dewight mumbled, "I'm... ah... yes. Yes, I'm Dewight Jones." Still in shock, he stood rigidly on the far side of the room and watched the Medi-bots load the dead husk of his wife onto a floating stretcher. Slowly, like moving a dinner cart full of spoiled food, the robots pushed the sheet out of the room. One of the Medi-bots straggled behind, dispensing a cue card from its open wrist and handing it to Dewight.

"Printed on this card is the information for the morgue in Greensboro where the body will be held. An extensive autopsy will be performed at the state's expense. Please contact the acting coroner before arranging any future burial services." Emotionless, as if talking to a sentient toaster, the Medi-bot added, "Sorry for your loss. Have a nice day." Its rubber slit of a mouth curved into an unnatural smile before joining the rest of its crew outside.

As the Medi-bots loaded Janis into the back of the ambulance and drove away, it finally dawned on Dewight. His best friend, his true love, was dead. Gone forever. Worst of all, the last time he would ever see Janis was of her wrapped up in a white sheet like a cheap Halloween costume.

I can't believe it... she's gone. My only friend... my soulmate. I'll never get to see that pretty smile or feel her warm skin against my own ever again. Oh God, this is all my fault. I should've done something... anything. Maybe... maybe I could've saved her somehow if I only knew–

It was the voice of the husky man standing at his side that brought Dewight back out of his endless string of morbid thoughts.

"I'm Sergeant William Morrow with the State Police. I'll be overseeing the investigation into your wife's death." Almost as an afterthought, he added, "I'm sorry for your loss, Mr. Jones, but I'll need to take your statement as to what exactly happened while my forensics team surveys the room for clues. Follow me, please." Forcing his head to nod feebly in compliance, Dewight followed Sgt. Morrow out into the living room as a stream of men in green shirts and rubber gloves stomped up and down the hallway.

Once in the living room, Morrow took a seat on the couch as Dewight settled into his favorite chair. Next to him, forever a reminder of what was lost, was Janis's empty recliner. The faint impression of her body in the worn cushioning caused tears to well up behind Dewight's eyes. Forcing his peripherals to push the unwanted reminder away, Dewight waited patiently as Morrow set up a pocket-size digital recorder on the coffee table between them.

"For continuity purposes, I'm going to record this interview. Any objection to that, Mr. Jones? Before you answer, I must remind you at this time that you are in no way under arrest. If you wish to decline this interview and request consultation, please say so now." Silently, Dewight shook his head. Seeing that Dewight was waiving his rights, Morrow turned on the device. "Alright," Morrow said, leaning back in his seat and crossing his arms over his chest, "why don't you start with the last time you saw your wife and work your way up to now, Mr. Jones."

Talking slow, making sure to recant every detail he could muster from his grief-stricken brain, Dewight told the Sgt. Morrow everything he needed to know.

Morrow sat patiently and listened to Dewight's story, nodding here and there when it felt appropriate. When Dewight reached the present, Morrow cleared his throat and asked, "So, you came home and found her unresponsive after being gone all day in... Bridgeton, was it?"

"Yeah, I was at Kurt Leavitt's farm all day. He sold me a new starter for my tractor."

Morrow nodded non-committedly. "Kurt Leavitt, he'll corroborate all of this?"

Dewight chuckled, the sound of his own voice sounding alien to his ears. "Oh yeah, he'll corroborate. Make sure when you talk to him you bring a sacked lunch, though. I swear that man's tongue is cut straight down the middle so it can wag both ways at the same time."

Morrow returned the short laugh, knowing exactly what Dewight meant. "I see. One of those busy talkers, huh? Thanks for the heads up." Morrow removed his phone from his breast pocket and quickly typed something before saying, "I'll be sending someone out there as soon as we are done here." Dewight watched as Morrow's faint smile faded to a look of concentrated concern. "What happened here?" he said, pointing one judgmental finger across the coffee table at Dewight's leg. Unsure of what Morrow meant, Dewight looked down curiously and saw that his right pantleg had a thick splotch of blood just over the knee.

"Oh... I don't know," Dewight said, picking at the now dried stain of reddish brown. He could feel the tingle of a small scab forming underneath his jeans, a fresh wound. "I must've cut my knee on a loose floorboard nail when I knelt at Janis's bedside. I guess I was so freaked out by everything going on that I didn't notice until now." Given the circumstances, Dewight didn't expect Morrow to readily believe this explanation, but was met with a surprising lack of suspicion.

"Thank you for your cooperation, Mr. Jones. This will conclude my interview," Morrow said dryly before leaning over and shutting off the recorder, stuffing it back into his front pocket. As he stood up briskly from the couch, he looked down at Dewight. "Just so you know, I don't think you had anything to do with your wife's death. I had dispatch run an extensive background check on you, came back clean. Call it a hunch, but you don't seem like the type to just get up one day and murder your wife of twenty years. Assuming your story checks out in Bridgeton, this will probably be the last time you'll see us here."

Unsatisfied, Dewight scoffed up grudgingly at Sgt. Morrow. "That's it? You're just going to get a statement from me and leave? That's bullshit! I need to know what happened to my wife! I need to know who did this!" Dewight shot up from his chair and stood tall in front of Morrow, chest heaving and fists clenched. As the two men locked eyes, glaring intensely at each other over the heat of the moment, a scrawny, bean pole of a man with rubber gloves on came running down the hallway into the living room.

"Sergeant! We found something."

Breaking the invisible chain of their glare, both Morrow and Dewight hurriedly followed the crime scene investigator back to the bedroom. Upon entering the room, a loose group of investigators could be seen crouching around the side of the now empty bed. Dewight realized that this was the very spot where he had dropped to his knees and cut himself. As they approached the group, Dewight could see tiny sparkles, like fractured diamonds, illuminating in the glow of flashlights on the wooden floorboards. Joining the loose circle, Morrow carefully knelt and inspected the mysterious glitter.

"Glass?" he asked the lead investigator as a woman in uniform carefully picked up the tiny slivers with a pair of steel tweezers. Cautiously, one by one, she dropped each individual piece into the open mouth of an evidence bag.

"Appears to be, sir. But we will test it back at the lab just to make sure." As the woman leaned forward to pick up a stray piece from under the end table, something caught her eye. Reaching under the small space with the tweezers, making sure not to come into contact with the broken shards and contaminating any potential evidence, she hooked the small object and pulled it out from the shadows. Slowly, everyone watched as she held up a U-shaped piece of stainless steel with two holes at each end.

"What the hell is that?" Dwight asked, completely perplexed by what he was looking at. No one answered his question as the lead investigator ordered another man to open another evidence bag so the piece could be catalogued separately. Dwight didn't know why, but an odd silence had come over the room just then. None of the investigators, including Sgt. Morrow, would acknowledge Dwight's question. Losing his patience once again, Dwight angrily stomped his foot and demanded, "Someone tell me right goddamn now what the that is?!"

Morrow was the first to say anything, rising from the floor and turning to face Dwight. With a heavy sigh, he said, "It's... It's S.A.M.A.N.T.H.A." Reading the puzzled look plastered on Dwight's face, Morrow laid a sturdy hand on his shoulder. "Join me outside for a smoke, and I'll explain everything you need to know. My crew won't be much longer. We'll be out of your hair soon enough, I promise."

Seeing no other choice, Dwight once again followed Sgt. Morrow like a lost puppy back down the hallway and out onto the front porch.

It took Morrow a long time to fully explain what the U-shaped nozzle and broken glass found in Dewight's house were. Morrow went over everything he could about Ubit Industries, even the recent rash of user deaths that had been ever present on every news platform. Dewight had plenty of questions, as Morrow thought he would. During this long conversation, he offered Dewight some of his nicotine cartridges as he talked, which Dewight readily denied every time. This didn't surprise Morrow. When doing a background check on Dewight Jones before arriving to the scene, Morrow was astonished to see the lack of information that was available. This ghostlike digital footprint could only mean one thing: Dewight was a Purist. Having never met one in the flesh before, Morrow thought it would only be right to fill him in on what was happening around the connected world. In Sgt. Morrow's mind, Janis had become just another statistic—an accidental death due to improper user upkeep. Morrow didn't come outright and say this to Dewight, but knew he would eventually grasp the concept. For now, he needed time to cope with the tragic loss first; logic would come later. When all technological questions were answered and Morrow was down to his last three vapor cartridges, Dewight was almost in tears. Head propped up by his strong hands on the arms of his wicker chair, the grieving husband tried hard to make sense of the whole thing.

After a long bout of silence, the chirping song of the crickets filling the night air, Dewight lifted his head and said, "This makes no sense. Janis would never go behind my back and use something so... so unnatural. Is there a possibility of foul play? Like, someone breaking into the house while I was gone and forcing Janis to become a user against her will?" The idea sounded crazy, even to a simplistic man like Dewight, but he was desperate for any kind of explanation that minimized Janis's direct involvement.

"Possibility? Yes, but not likely," Morrow answered honestly. "Every person has to accept the terms of service warning upon entering the program. If Janis were forced to ingest S.A.M.A.N.T.H.A. against her will, she could've easily declined the terms and come back."

Dewight vaguely understood, but still couldn't believe what he was hearing. Continuing to grasp at straws, he added, "There's no way she could've bought this shit not knowing what it was, could she? Janis just got one of those tablet things not too long ago... is it possible she got bored with it and tried to upgrade?"

Morrow took a second to consider this before saying, "I suppose. I think all Ubit outlet stores sell canisters of S.A.M.A.N.T.H.A."

"Even the one in town? The used electronics store across the street from the market?"

"I believe so, yes." Knowing intuitively what Dewight was driving at, Morrow quickly added, "But don't go looking for answers down there. Like I said, there's been a string of unexplained deaths connected with the program. This thing— this company—reaches across the entire world. Ubit has already addressed the issue publicly, blaming user malware for the deaths, not the product itself."

Refusing to look Morrow in the eye, Dewight rubbed at his chin with grease-stained fingertips and looked off into the night. "User malware, huh? Sounds like a fleece job to me."

Morrow chuckled, his trained eye watching Dewight intently through the thin cloud of cinnamon flavored mist escaping his parted lips. He knew he had to tread lightly now and not give the man any wild ideas. "Maybe, maybe not. All I know is that there's no sense in chasing windmills trying find your wife's killer, Mr. Jones. I know you don't want to hear this... but the horrible truth is that sometimes awful things happen to the best of us. *Accidents* happen. It's very likely that Janis was a new user and didn't follow the proper system protocols and ended up paying with her life. I know that's a tough pill to swallow, but you need to be open to that possibility."

When Dewight said nothing, only continued to stare out vacantly at the sleeping hillside, Morrow stood from his chair and again laid a firm hand on Dewight's shoulder. "We'll still be carrying out a full investigation, you can set your watch to that. All the evidence will be tested, no stone left unturned. If there is any evidence of foul play, as you suggested, I won't hesitate to hunt the person—or persons—responsible down. You have my word on that. But, if the tests come back the other way, that your wife's death was accidental, you need to be ready for that possibility. Some questions don't have answers, Mr. Jones. The sooner you come to terms with that, the easier it will be to go on with your life."

Leaving Dewight on the front porch, Sgt. Morrow reentered the house. His team was in the midst of packing up their gear. Within minutes, they were coming down the hallway single file like a row of toy ducks in big shiny boots. One by one, they got in their squad cars and drove away. Sgt. Morrow was the last to leave, making sure to wish Dewight a good night and letting him know that he would personally be in touch once the investigation neared a close. As a sign of mutual understanding, Morrow offered his hand to Dewight on the front porch, but was met with nothing. Just as before, Dewight continued to sit silently, his dark-ringed eyes never leaving the swaying trees on the edge of the distant forest.

As Sgt. Morrow got into his car and pulled out of the long dirt driveway, he couldn't help feeling that he'd be seeing Dewight Jones a lot sooner than he'd like to.

I've seen that look before, Morrow thought to himself as he traveled the long country road back to the station. *That's the look of a man who demands answers, even when there aren't any to give. And, God willing, he'll find what he's looking for. At any cost necessary.*

CHAPTER 7

At the sight of the rising sun beginning to peek over the pointed roof of the barn, Dewight Jones finally stood up stiffly from his wicker chair on the front porch. Bones creaking and joints tight like old rubber gaskets, he had to quickly reach out and catch himself on the wood railing as his body began to teeter. Clutching the paint chipped railing to keep himself from falling over, Dewight felt incredibly fragile; weaker than he'd ever felt in his entire life. He hadn't slept much that night, mostly passing out from mental exhaustion in little spurts here and there. When Dewight's eyelids became too heavy to keep open, he was forced to revisit Janis's wax mannequin corpse; her eyes wide open and mouth turned down in a frown as he stood weightless at their bedside. Her hair, just as wild and golden as it had always been, flowed like an aura of light around her head and shoulders.

Why did you let me die? those glassy eyes would say, her phantom words shallow and breathless like the dry rustle of autumn leaves. Even in his tainted dreams, Janis's perfect lips would never move again. *Why, snoogy woogums? Why didn't you save me? I thought you loved me...*

As if struck by a stray bolt of lightning, Dewight would be jolted back to consciousness several times from the massive shock of guilt he felt from those words. Beads of cold sweat clinging the thin lining of dirty work clothes to his damp skin, the *thump-thump* of his own broken heart would momentarily blot out any sounds of the surrounding night. Each time Dewight would come back from that bedside, he'd pray to the dead light of the distant stars above that the whole ordeal had been some kind of terrible nightmare.

"No, she's in the house right now, sound asleep in bed. Has to be," Dewight would tell himself, speaking his twisted logic out loud to the sleeping cattle in an attempt to filter some of the awful thoughts that swirled endlessly like a whirlpool in his head. "This can't be happening. It just can't."

But when he'd force his tired eyes down to his aching right knee, that dark brown stain of blood reminded him that the past was set in stone. Janis was dead, and nothing was going to bring her back. Unable to go back into the house, unable to face the emptiness that was now his life, Dewight just sat on the front porch and tried to collect his thoughts.

At first, he couldn't think about much. The strange mixture of vengeful rage and immeasurable sorrow he felt kept him away from any kind of linear thinking. But as the minutes melted into hours, his head began to clear of the emotional fog. And as the world slowly turned to face the light of the sun once again, so did Dewight's mind. The toxic anger and guilt slowly dissolved away, and what was left was a narrow determination to find the truth. Dewight knew himself well. He knew he couldn't just sit here and twiddle his thumbs while Sgt. Morrow ran endless tests. He knew the results would never come back with a full explanation for Janis's death, leaving more questions than answers. It was impossible for Dewight to imagine a life without Janis. For almost twenty years, they'd been virtually inseparable— physically and spiritually tethered to one another. Losing Janis felt to Dewight like losing an irreplaceable piece of himself. Half of his heart and soul.

Trying hard to come to terms with the cruel reality of his situation, Dewight narrowed down his options. Shamefully, suicide was one of the first avenues to present itself. He thought about it a lot that night, and for a while it seemed like a viable choice. In his mind's eye, he saw himself just getting up from that wicker chair, walking into the house, and grabbing the hunting rifle from under the loose floorboards in the living room. Traveling down that long hallway for the last time, he'd sit in the same spot on the bed were his wife's corpse had been only hours earlier. Without a word, Dewight would remove one shoe and sock. Looping his big toe around the spring-loaded trigger on the other end of the gun, he'd close his eyes and put the cold steel in his mouth. Keeping only thoughts of Janis in the front of his mind, Dewight would slowly apply pressure until... *BANG!*

Problem solved.

Only, he knew deep down that it wouldn't be that simple. Dewight wasn't afraid to die, far from it. What his conscious had a problem with was the fact that he was taking the easy way out. The part of him that hurt so badly from the loss of his beloved wife just wanted the pain to end, but an even bigger part of him—that one that screamed for vengeance—told him something different.

If you're going to die, that spiteful voice rose up through the depressive muck and shouted at him in his head, *then do it avenging Janis's death. You owe her that much. Don't take the coward's way out, she wouldn't have wanted it that way. You know it in your heart of hearts to be true.*

By the time the warm rays of the sun pushed away the resting gloom of sterile night, Dewight had made up his mind. Hands still tight on the porch railing, he allowed his body to adjust before letting go. Finding much needed balance, Dewight pulled out his phone and made a call to Kurt Leavitt.

"Kurt? Yeah, it's Dewight. Dewight Jones. Listen, I need a favor," Dewight said, not allowing Kurt to butt in with any small talk. "I'm coming by your place... yeah, now. What? I don't care what time it is! Listen to me, I'm coming down there to buy every single piece of steel and bolts you got for sale. I'll pay you double for whatever you got."

Kurt immediately understood the code words Dewight was using for guns and bullets. Thanks to the efforts of many high-ranking members of congress over the past several decades, personal possession of firearms had been all but outlawed. Too much media flak from mass shootings and domestic terrorists over the years finally pushed the collective consciousness of the country over the edge. People were scared out of their wits and were demanding drastic solutions. But the ol' US of A was too far down the rabbit hole for the powers that be to just outright change the Second Amendment and take everyone's guns away. That move was more than a little risky, possibly sparking a second civil war. In an effort to avoid this outcome and still meet everyone halfway, tight guidelines and mandatory registrations were soon put into place. This came in the form of heavy monitorization, documentation, and regulations enforced by the government. Since 2038, it was illegal for any U.S. citizen to own or sell an undocumented weapon of any kind, violation punishable by a minimum of fifteen years in prison.

So, just like the early days of prohibition, tens of thousands of people turned to the black market to meet their needs and avoid being listed on a government database. Dewight knew Kurt owned secret guns as well, buying them privately in shady backroom deals such as he did. Despite this common interest, Dewight could hear Kurt's apprehensiveness to this request on the other end of the call. But, after several moments of incoherent mumbling, Dewight eventually got the response he was looking for. "Thanks, Kurt. Have everything ready, I'll be there soon." He then hung up before Kurt could attempt to gab or stall any further.

With newfound strength and determination, Dewight charged into the house and went straight to the bedroom to begin packing. Finding two of his old duffle bags buried deep in the closet, he frantically emptied his dresser drawers into one bag until it swelled with clean clothes. The next stop on his way back down the hall was the living room where he unloaded the contents of his stashed guns and loose cash into the other bag, making sure to pick every stray bullet and crumpled bill out of the dirt. He already had a heavy salvo—two semi-automatic pistols, a double barrel shotgun, and a long-range hunting rifle—but with Kurt's added weaponry, he should have more than enough to execute his plan. Both heavy bags in hand, he kicked his way out the door and shambled out to his truck. Loading the bags into the cab behind the seats, Dewight then jumped in and cranked the engine to life. But, just as soon as he threw it into gear, something inside told him to stop.

Go back. You're forgetting something.

Unsure at first what his intuition was trying to tell him, Dewight let the truck idle for a moment before killing the engine and jumping back out into the dirt. Climbing back up the porch steps, he ran into the kitchen and grabbed the fully charged tablet off the table. He'd be needing it later if the first part of his plan didn't fail.

Don't forget the charger, that calm, logical voice said. Anxiously, he looked around the room but saw no sign of it. Remembering that Janis sometimes kept it in her purse, Dewight ran into the hallway and scooped the pastel bag off its peg on the coat rack. It hurt to do so, but Dewight opened the purse and glanced inside. Along with the charger, there were all of Janis's stray candies, tiny trinkets, and make-up accessories. The familiar smell of red roses drifted up from the belly of the bag, bringing a tear to Dewight's eye. Slowly, he reached in for the charger, but stopped when that cool and collective voice spoke up again.

Take the bag. You never know what you might need in there somewhere down the road.

Despite not immediately seeing the logic in carrying around his dead wife's purse, Dewight ultimately decided not to argue with himself. Purse in hand, he headed back out to the truck and tossed it in the cab with the rest of the bags. Tires spitting clouds of dust into the bright morning light, he sped out of the driveway and off towards Bridgeton.

Dewight didn't know it yet, but that would be the last time he'd ever step foot on his family farm ever again.

***

Kurt Leavitt was initially excited to strike up a conversation with Dewight when he stopped by the farm that morning. Foaming at the mouth to bend someone's ear, he had a whole host of questions and comments to run by his fair-weather friend. Still unaware of Janis's death the prior night, Kurt thought Dewight's urgent visit was due to some sort of personal troubles outside the home, possibly business related.

'Haps a bad cattle trade? Rotten feed deal? he wondered longingly over his morning cup of joe. Anxiously waiting, Kurt kept one greasy eye out the kitchen window for any sign of Dewight's dusty old pickup as he sipped at the mug full of bitter black juice. Them Douglas brothers is always tryin' tah put the screws to some poor bastard. I warned 'em, he can't say I din't. Nope. No, siree. Can't trus' nobody dee's days.

Heading a trail of rising dust, Kurt finally saw Dewight's pickup tearing up the road. Within seconds of seeing it, the pickup roared into the driveway and skidded to a stop. If Dewight had hit the brakes any later, Kurt's chicken coop would've been flattened under his front tires. Giddy with unwarranted yarns to spin, Kurt jumped from his chair and ran out to the driveway to meet Dewight. But, as Kurt crossed the driveway, he caught a glimpse of the haggard face and wild eyes behind the wheel and stopped. Remarkably, maybe for the first time since he learned to spit words, Kurt decided to keep his big mouth shut. Instead of the friendly visit he was hoping for, the two men just did a little bit of business and parted ways, simple as that. Adding another pistol and ten boxes of ammo to his arsenal, Dewight forked over part of his fat wad of cash to a very confused Kurt and promptly left without a word. No explanation was given to the sudden purchase, and Kurt somehow knew better than to ask for one. He might not have been a terribly bright man by any stretch of the imagination, but even Kurt Leavitt knew that something was wrong with Dewight Jones that morning. He wasn't his usual chummy self. The Dewight that Kurt met that morning was darker, full of quiet determination that could be felt like radiating heat from a distance. Needless to say, Kurt knew that trouble was brewing. And whatever that trouble might be, he didn't dare to get mixed up in it.

"He looked like hell on wheels," Kurt would later be quoted telling reporters, police, and alike once the truth finally came out about Dewight's master plan. "I ain't never seen nobody with dat look of pure hatred in their eyes. Never. No, siree. I din't know what dun it, but that man was out fer blood. An' I ain't fittin to be the first in line fer dat."

* * *

After his trip to Bridgeton, Dewight turned around and headed straight back to Kittery. It was nearing noon when he reached the outskirts of town where the bumpy dirt roads turned to smooth lines of sealed pavement. In minutes, he was cruising down Main Street; the giant digital sign for the used electronics store hanging like a giant exclamation point in the horizon. Pulling into the empty parking lot, Dewight took a couple of minutes to play with the tablet. He was hoping he'd find the info he needed online and not have to go into the store at all. But after minutes of scrolling through endless pages of neon distractions, Dewight got frustrated and gave up, tossing it onto the empty passenger seat to his right. Taking a quick moment to breathe, Dewight then loaded the full clip into his new Glock 18 and shoved it into his front pocket.

This is the first step, he thought anxiously, his nerves tight but not at all rattled. *Just get the info you need and get out of there. Don't hurt anyone unless you have to. Remember, this is for Janis.*

With her name ringing like church bells between his ears, Dewight got out of the truck and entered the store. Walking slowly through the aisles, the electric eyes of sleeping machinery carrying his distorted reflection like the eyes of a giant spider, he eventually came across the same face that Janis had seen the day she unknowingly purchased her one-way ticket to death's door.

Standing in a corner behind a rack of VR Goggles, the pudgy, flesh-stained clerk looked up from his phone and acknowledged his first potential customer of the day. "Welcome to Ubit Electronics—Home to all your used electronic needs. My name is Darrin. How may I help you today?"

Forcing a friendly smile to his face, Dewight hooked his thumbs in the front pockets of his faded jeans and said, "Yeah... I'm, uh... looking for S.A.M.A.N.T.H.A."

Returning the smile, with just a hint of credulity tucked in the crusty corners of his mouth, Darrin motioned for Dewight to follow him as he waddled over to the counter. Dipping down behind the glass countertop, Darrin brought out a small white box. Lifting the lid slowly, as if whatever lay inside were highly combustible, Darrin laid the box open and turned it readily towards Dewight. Lined in neat rows, cushioned by a fine layer of Styrofoam and bubble wrap, laid twenty or so vials full of lazy blue mist. Dewight remained silent as he gazed upon the mysterious contraptions, eyes studying the hazy tubes of swirling turquoise. Dewight immediately recognized the visual allure of the product; its sleek design and harmless appearance made it appear docile, almost comforting in a way. No more harmless than a sugary drink or head of blue cotton candy, this was just another product for mass consumption. This allusive factor reignited that first spark of vengeful rage behind Dewight's eyes.

"How many you need?" Darrin asked, starting to become uncomfortable with Dewight's cold silence. He kept his hands just under the backside of the counter, one finger resting next to the panic button that sent a direct call to the police. Once activated, every door and window in the building would lock shut until the authorities arrived. Darrin didn't know Dewight's intentions but had read plenty of stories online about desperate users robbing these types of stores for a quick fix. S.A.M.A.N.T.H.A. was easily affordable to anyone, Ubit made sure of that, but the primal instinct of human greed that surges in all of God's creatures made some people do unreasonable things to get back online.

Usually, thieves would steal a couple boxes of vials and either use them, squirreling them away for personal use, or sell them in bulk on the black market. But, in the recent years, a different kind of motive had been trending more and more. Members of the P.H.R.G. —Purist's Human Rights Group—would stage faux robberies, but they wouldn't clean out the store's supply for a profit or glutenous use. Instead, they'd destroy every vial, making sure no one had a chance to use them. The P.H.R.G. was an infamous anti-tech radical group that violently resisted the modern advances put forth by Ubit Industries. Darrin had never met anyone belonging to said group, but judging by Dewight's rustic look and emotionless smile, he thought chances were good that he might be standing in the presence of one.

"Yeah... I, uh... I'll take three," Dewight finally said, his words flat and throat unbearably dry. Fingers still hooked in his pockets, he felt the hard handle of the gun with the back of his hand and quickly gathered his thoughts. "Can I ask you something?" Dewight asked as Darrin began bagging up his purchase. "Where do these things come from?"

Pausing, Darrin looked up from the half-wrapped package and scanned Dewight's face. "Sir?" He didn't like where this transaction was going. The more he thought about it, the more this seemed like one of those dreaded scenarios that he had read so much about online. Not wanting to lose his cool and prompt any unnecessary action, Darrin continued to play the role of malleable store clerk, his shaky hand once again drifting back to the hidden button under the counter.

"I'm just curious," Dewight assured, feeling the clerk's unease at his inquiry. "Where do they make this stuff? Is there a distribution center or factory that pumps it out somewhere close to here?" Using Janis's tablet in the parking lot, Dewight had attempted to get this information online, but didn't find much of anything. Aside from the locations of outlet stores in the area, Ubit Technologies kept the location of their manufacturing plants under wraps. Dewight knew it was a long shot, but he hoped that maybe a store employee would have some inside information that he could use later. But, judging by the sour stare that Darrin was giving him, Dewight knew his plan was off to a bad start.

"I'm not at liberty to discuss Ubit business strategies with customers. Company policy, sir."

This open-ended comment started a wheel of logical thought in Dewight's head.

He does know something. It might not be much, but it's something. You need to get any info you can if you want to carry on with your plan. The memory of Janis can't stop here. You knew the risk that might come from this, or else you wouldn't be standing here with a loaded gun in your pocket.

Without thinking, Dewight whipped the gun out and steadied it at the clerk's fat head. "Fuck the company policy. Tell me what you know, or I'll spray your brain all over that back wall."

Darrin froze, too scared to move or speak. His finger rested right next to the panic button but was too stiff to move. His tendons felt like steel cable, ready to snap under the surge of fear that rushed through him. Gun still leveled at Darrin's face, Dewight shouted, "Speak!"

"Alright alright, calm down, sir," Darrin said, dread making his voice sound shaky and uneven. "There's cameras everywhere in here. They are watching us right now." Moving only his eyes, Darrin looked to the corners of the room at the black bulbs. "This isn't worth whatever you're after—"

"Shut up!" Dewight screamed, jumping Darrin on his feet. "You have no idea what I lost because of this shit!" With his other hand, Dewight swept the open box of vials onto the floor, where they shattered. A thin blue mist rose briefly from the pile of broken glass before dissipating back into the air. "Start talking before I lose my patience."

With a hard gulp, Darrin said, "Listen, the company doesn't tell me anything. I swear. I'm just a salesman. I get a full shipment in every week from a trucking company that corporate sets up—"

"Shipment? Shipment from where?"

"I don't know. The figureheads in corporate are in charge of all the—" Darrin's words were cut short when the tip of the gun was brought closer to his face. Feeling the cold kiss of the steel against his sweat laced forehead suddenly changed his tune. On the verge of tears, he blurted, "Portland."

"Speak up!"

"Portland! They come from a guarded factory in Portland!" Darrin began to blubber, fresh tears sliding down the surface of his oily skin and collecting under the fold of his double chin.

"How do I know you're not lying and just trying to save your own ass?" Dewight asked skeptically, keeping his finger rested lightly over the trigger.

"I'm only telling you what the driver told me. I don't know if it's true or not. He showed me his security clearance card once, the guy's a real blowhard. Always bragging about the top secret shit he gets to see when he does his runs."

Dewight held the gun up for several more seconds before slowly lowering it back to his side. "Portland, huh? Alright, thanks…" for the first time since entering the store, Dewight looked down at the clerk's name tag and added, "Darrin." Getting what he needed, Dewight turned and walked briskly down the aisle towards the exit.

Finally let go from his stasis of fear, Darrin wiped the salty tears from his cheeks and searched for the panic button under the counter. As his finger laid over it, slowly applying pressure, his mind screamed out at him.

No! Let him go! If you lock him in here, he'll kill you for sure! You saw his eyes!

Watching Dewight strut confidently down the aisleway, every long step bringing him closer to the exit, Darrin wrestled with corporate protocol and his own sense of self-preservation. But, by the time Darrin made a decision to abide by company policy, Dewight was already out the door and walking to his pickup. Collapsing into a ball of quivering goop behind the counter, Darrin hated himself for being such a spineless coward. What he had to do next was almost as bad as getting shot in the face.

Slipping his phone from his pocket, Darrin found the only number he never wished to see and pressed call. In less than five rings, he was on a direct line to a corporate representative for Ubit Industries. Darrin wished so badly now that he had died like a hero, at least then he wouldn't have to face the awful punishment that lay ahead. Ubit Industries would pull all the surveillance footage, seeing that Darrin had not only broken protocol, but divulged valuable company information to an armed lunatic. Things looked bad for him, but Darrin prayed that this call would absolve him of some sort of guilt. Besides, the higher-ups might have their hands full for a little while. Or, at least until they caught up with Dewight in Portland.

"Yeah, this is Darrin McDougal, Kittery location... we have a big problem."

CHAPTER 8

Dr. Smith was sitting quietly in her office, chair turned towards the giant glass windows overseeing the city, when the intercom on her desk buzzed to life.

"Excuse me, Doctor," the sheepish voice said, "a representative from the United Nations is here to see you."

Watching the little ant-people run their busy little grid down below, Dr. Smith sighed heavily before turning back to her desk. Pressing the intercom button, she said, "Send him in." Within seconds, a wiry looking man in a dark suit strode in through the doors and approached her desk.

"Hello, Dr. Smith," the man said, his soft face and shiny black hair shifting slightly at every syllable. "I am here on behalf of the United Nations to discuss the ongoing matter of—"

"Jesus Christ, they couldn't send a real person to come talk to me?" Dr. Smith said, rolling her eyes at the sight of yet another subservient robot. She knew they'd be sending one, they almost always did, but that didn't stop her from teasing and taunting them for their cowardice efforts at collecting information. "I assume they are watching right now. Hiding behind their long desks and cheesy name plates, yes?"

The robot in peach colored skin blinked twice then said, "Yes. Our meeting is being transmitted live back to my superiors through 40k resolution optic lenses in my—"

"Shut up, you fancy can opener," Dr. Smith interjected. "Let's just get this over with. I'm very busy, as I'm sure you and your puppet masters already know."

Unable to feel slighted by the doctor's rude comments, the suited robot pulled the corners of it mouth up into a smile and said, "I am here to discuss the recent onslaught of deaths involving S.A.M.A.N.T.H.A."

"Of course you are. And as I told the U.N. on the phone yesterday, I got all my best people on it trying to solve the issue. We are almost there, but we need a little more time. What else do you need to know?"

"The problem is escalating, Doctor, and the world leaders are having a hard time explaining this away to their people. The various media outlets are now being told a different story from what Ubit has initially released. It seems that members of the P.H.R.G. are strategically leaking information to the press that the recent deaths are caused by the program itself and not the—"

Dr. Smith slammed both her hands flat on her desk, raising herself out of her chair like a praying mantis. "Those nosey Neanderthals don't know shit! I told you already, this issue isn't internal, it's a user error. As long as people follow the recommended scans and checks, they'll be fine." Smoothing out a few wrinkles in her blouse, Dr. Smith lowered back into her chair and resumed a more pleasant tone. "Now, I know they didn't send you all the way down here just to ask me what everyone already knows. So?"

The robot flinched slightly, as if even its soldered veins could feel the bitter coldness from her stare. "I've been instructed to tour the facility. As things stand, we could very well be facing a global epidemic unlike anything ever seen. Did you know that in the last two days, over six hundred casualties have been reported worldwide?"

Smiling, lips painted blood red, Dr. Smith pretended to check a stack of papers on her desk before saying, "Hmm... no, I didn't get that information yet. Must've slipped past one of my secretaries this morning while I was down in the research lab. I'll be sure to note it now." Plucking a gold-plated pen from the edge of her desk, she leaned forward and scribbled FUCK YOU on one of the pieces of paper before folding it neatly and placing it in the top drawer of her desk. "There. Noted."

"Dr. Smith!" the robot suddenly screeched, its voice completely different than before. Dr. Smith quickly realized that whoever was watching on the other end of the live feed was using the robot as a moving intercom. "Stop this right now! There are hundreds of people dying every minute from your creation! We demand that you let us tour your research facility as to better understand what the—"

A marble paperweight shaped like a Griffin flew across the room and collided with the robot's skull, cutting off the rest of the message. Bolts and fake skin exploded from the dapper android as his body swayed then crashed to the ground. Spasming on the floor, bright sparks and tails of smoke rising from the massive crater in its face, shattered words and phrases still tried to escape from its flapping metallic jaw.

"… is enough! We… vernment sanctions… to stand down imme… unishable by law!"

Still smiling, Dr. Smith rose from her desk. Heels clicking on the hard floor, she crossed the room and stood over the twitching figure. Making sure it's one good eye was focused on her, she knelt down close. "She's mine. You hear me? I made her, it's my call. None of you can tell me what to do. I am above the law; I am above all of you. This ends when I say it ends. Goodbye."

With the pointed heel of her shoe, Dr. Smith drove the spike straight down into the remaining eye. Puncturing clear through to its circuit board brain, the android let out one final spasm before laying still on the floor. Pulling her foot out of the collapsed skull, Dr. Smith sat back down at her desk and pressed the intercom button.

"Susan, send a cleanup crew in here now to pick up this mess."

"Yes, Dr. Smith," the nervous voice said. As Dr. Smith brushed away the loose bangs from her face, that anxiously tight voice came back. "Oh… I also have a message for you that just came in from the Northeast division."

"Yeah yeah, I know. Tell them that I already talked to the U.N. and that they know—"

"No," Susan interrupted, immediately regretting doing so. "It's… it's not about that."

"Then what? Out with it!"

The small voice hesitated, almost too scared to speak. "There's… there's been a security breach at one of the stores. An armed man asking questions about the company. The person or persons involved are believed to be heading to the distribution center in Portland as we speak."

Against all odds, this added element didn't bother Dr. Smith at all. As calmly as she had been while watching the specks of body flow in and out of the tiny streets, she hit the intercom button and said, "Pass a message along to the security stationed at the Portland facility, ASAP. If anyone, and I mean anyone, attempts to enter the grounds without proper authorization… kill them. Understood?"

"Yes, Dr. Smith."

The intercom again fell silent as Dr. Smith turned back to the busy street below and continued her God-like observation of the ants.

CHAPTER 9

    Head buzzing and gut grumbling, Dewight peeled down Route 2 with his hands gripped tight on the worn leather of the steering wheel. The adrenaline of pulling a gun on that store clerk gave him a high that put pins and needles to the soles of his feet as he pushed the gas pedal. Metal to the floor, his old truck roared through the desolate countryside like an angry tiger chasing after an invisible gazelle through the bush. He felt immense urgency in every curve and bump that passed on the road under him. His internal clock ticking to the pace of his racing heart, Dewight was frantic to beat the odds stacked against him and fulfill the only goal left in his life that held any purpose.

    With Janis gone, taken from him by the modern man's sinful invention of electric junk, there was now nothing left here on this Earth to take solace in. Nothing, except swift and rightful vengeance. This intense drive to avenge the only woman he ever loved pushed Dewight along like the unseen finger of God. To his calculations, the nearest Ubit manufacturing facility, supposedly located in the bustling metropolis of Portland, was nearly three hundred miles away. Despite this relatively close distance, Dewight had serious concerns of what exactly he should do next.

I have a feeling that they'll be expecting me now, Dewight thought, remembering the many cameras that undoubtedly recorded everything he did while inside the used electronics store. The clerk had said that the company was monitoring them, but Dewight was too amped up at that moment to ever take that factor into consideration when initiating the first phase of his plan. He hoped now that this lack of oversight wouldn't sink his ship before he even had a chance to leave the harbor. *Either way... the cops will be looking for me. I seriously doubt that clerk just went about his day and didn't call me in to the cops.* Driving along, houses no more than squared blurs that ran like wet paint past his side window, Dewight came to the logical conclusion that he had to try and lay low if he wanted to make it into the city. Hauling ass across the state like a bat out of Hell was sure to get someone's attention, no matter how many back roads he took. Avoiding contact with the cops was Dewight's number one priority. With the cab full of unregistered guns, there was bound to be a standoff—if or when that time came. Dewight couldn't promise himself that he would shoot his way out of custody but knew that if it was what it took to avenge Janis's death, then so be it. He hadn't stolen anything from the store, but the brandishing of an unregistered weapon was enough to get him mandatory prison time, not to mention the box of vials he broke in his fit of rage. Calming himself down and forcing logic to take the wheel, Dewight's foot slowly eased up off the gas pedal. Against his urge to exact revenge as quickly as possible, he knew that in order to do that he'd have to think ahead.

There should be another town coming up in the next couple miles, his logic dictated, pushing the thoughts of suicide by cop out of Dewight's head. *Pull over and get some food in you. You haven't eaten anything in almost 24 hours. Find a quiet place off the main road and keep your head down. The cops are probably up at the farm looking for you at this very moment, that should bide you a little bit more time. But don't get too comfortable.*

Listening to his head and his empty gut, Dewight coasted along at a more comfortable speed. Nervously, he checked his rearview mirror every thirty seconds or so, praying that the flashing lights of a state trooper wouldn't pop up behind him.

As he crossed the town line into Yelk—a sleepy little ghost town, almost identical to Kittery—Dewight followed the weather-stripped signs to a little diner called Sal's Place. Just as he had hoped, it was a modest tin roofed building that sat obscurely between a condemned antiques store and a junk covered scrap yard. There was only a single car in the gravel parking lot on the far side of the diner; a mud caked Jeep with a canvas top and heavy treaded tires. Using the only other vehicle as partial camouflage, Dewight pulled in on the other side of the Jeep so anyone driving by wouldn't be able to see his truck fully.

Once parked, Dewight anxiously opened the driver's side door, one foot out on the loose gravel, but then stopped. Looking around to make sure no one was watching, he tucked the handgun that lay on the passenger seat into the front of his belt and tucked in his shirt over it.

You can't be too safe now. Everything you once knew has changed... always be prepared. Always.

With those paranoid words rattling around in his head, Dewight exited his truck and casually entered the diner.

Surprisingly, he felt a small amount of nostalgic comfort when he stepped inside of the modestly furnished restaurant. With cracked leather booths lining the grease stained walls, a long slab of paint-chipped counter that separated the closed kitchen from the small dining area, and an ancient jukebox collecting dust in a corner by the bathroom, the otherwise drab interior was pleasantly underwhelming. Though the location of the diner was rustic, Dewight had expected to see something modern. He expected to see electric tickers and impossibly flat televisions covering every wall, polished chrome and bleeding lights lining every hard edge and corner. Feeling a little bit safer in a place so clearly out of touch with the times, Dewight took a seat in a booth by the jukebox and began looking through a menu.

That little bit of excitement he felt was short lived, though, as he browsed the limited food choices. It had been a well-known fact for many years that real meat was a commodity, reserved for those who were lucky enough to have a farming license or the funds to spend $500 on a single piece of rubbery steak. Because of the excessive amounts of methane that most livestock produced, farming was closely regulated by the powers that be. Mass production of all meat products—from beef to chicken—was banned, deemed too harmful for the already fragile eco-system. Plant-based substitutes were now the norm, promising the same taste, texture, and sustenance of the real thing. Most people went along with it, either out of environmental consciousness or lack of choice. In the end, everyone needed to eat something, and soon forgot what made the real thing so important.

But those with certain credentials were allowed to have the minimal amount of livestock necessary to sustain themselves. These licenses were almost impossible to obtain, but because Dewight came from a long line of highly respected ranchers, he was allowed to continue the tradition of his forefathers on a much smaller scale if he vowed not to exceed the government sanctioned limit on cattle. This lineage had granted him the luxury of never having to eat any kind of plant-based substitute. The very idea made his empty stomach clench together like a fist, sending sharp jolts of pain through his abdomen.

This isn't the time for your Holier than thou bullshit. This isn't a matter of pride or principle; this is about survival. You need to eat, now. Just pick something, fill up your gut, and get the fuck out of here. You need to get as far away from Kittery as you can before nightfall. Remember, they're coming.

Just as this reminder hit home for Dewight in the form a massive stomach cramp, an elderly woman in a gravy stained apron approached his booth. Pen and pad in hand, she looked down at Dewight disinterestedly with her heavily mascaraed eyes and said, "What can I getcha, hun?"

Not bothering to look through the menu again, Dewight sighed heavily, one hand rubbing absently at his aching stomach. "What would you recommend?"

"It's all the same shit," the wrinkled waitress said bluntly with a catty sneer, "but if I had to eat here, I'd get the meatloaf. It ain't what my momma used to make, but it isn't half bad. Comes with a side of mashed potatoes and seasoned green beans."

Against his better judgment, Dewight asked, "Are the sides made fresh, at least?"

Hand resting on her lumpy hip, the waitress let out a smoker's cackle at Dewight's ignorance before saying, "Honey, ain't nothin' made fresh no more. It's all shipped in frozen from only God knows where. Probably not even grown in the ground. They make everything in labs nowadays. Tastes damn near the same with the right amount of seasoning, though, if you ask me."

You wouldn't know prime rib from an old leather shoe, Dewight thought sorely to himself, trying not let his rising irritation show. Keeping his pessimism inside, he ordered the meatloaf and a cup of black coffee. After the waitress left his booth and disappeared behind the counter, Dewight stood up and examined the jukebox that sat to his left. Upon closer inspection, he wasn't surprised to see that it wasn't a real jukebox, but actually an outdated computer with a retro casing. Dewight stared at the black screen, his dim reflection fuzzed by a thick layer of dust. Without thinking, he reached out and wiped his fingers across the screen. The dry dust felt gritty on his fingertips, like grey sand. Needing to wash the dirt off his hands before he ate, Dewight turned from the dead machine and began to walk towards the bathroom. As he turned, a solemn figure became caught in his peripherals, causing him to stop mid-step.

There, sitting at the far end of the counter next to the bathroom, was a woman dressed in baggy cargo pants and a camouflage jacket. Her long chestnut colored hair was tied up in a loose ponytail, pulled through the hole of a wide brimmed trucker hat. Hands curled around a cup of steaming coffee, she held her gaze on Dewight for only a moment before looking back down at the counter in solemn silence.

Was she there when I walked in? Dewight asked himself as he tried to keep his stride to the bathroom at a natural pace. He was so distracted by everything else going on in his head that he couldn't remember. Tendons tight like steel cable, Dewight quickly walked the short length to the bathroom and went inside. Once the door was locked behind him, he took his time washing his hands, trying hard to calm his nerves.

Stay calm. She's just another customer, no different than you. Probably the owner of the Jeep you parked behind outside. Nothing to freak out about. If you start acting up now, the waitress will get spooked and call in the cavalry to come pick you up. Just sit down, eat, and get on your way. There's nothing to be wary of... yet.

Splashing cold water on his face and mopping it dry with the stiff paper towel from the dispenser, Dewight continued to push his anxieties onto the back burner of his mind. Once he collected his bearings, he walked out of the bathroom and back into the dining area to his booth. On his way back, he noticed the woman with the trucker cap wasn't at the counter anymore, her abandoned cup of coffee the only proof of her ever being there. Sitting down in his booth, Dewight was about to dip back into the already brimming pot of anxiety when the aging waitress came out from behind the counter with his coffee and food.

Distracted by the aroma wafting in from the swinging door of the kitchen, Dewight said, "Wow, that was fast."

"Don't take long to heat up what's already been cooked, honey," she snarked, setting down the loaded plate in front of him. As she set down the mug of coffee by the jar of powdered creamer to his right, she gingerly added, "Enjoy." With that, the waitress returned to the secret solidarity of the back room to let Dewight eat alone in peace.

Fork in hand, Dewight began to examine his food hesitantly, amazed at how familiar its presentation was. From every angle, it looked just like the real thing, right down to the gristle on the beef. Knowing that he didn't have time to play food critic, Dewight filled up his fork and began shoveling. Bite after bite, he felt the gnawing in his gut begin to dissipate. He didn't care much for the flavor of the faux food, or lack thereof, but had to admit to himself that it was much better than he had anticipated. Cleaning his entire plate in under ten minutes, Dewight finally felt content and leaned back in his booth to let his body digest.

As he sipped his coffee, the waitress came by and dropped off the check. The meal was surprisingly cheap, another benefactor to eating only processed food. After paying the check and leaving a tip, Dewight downed the rest of his coffee while it was still warm, collected his receipt, and stepped back out into the parking lot. Walking quickly towards his truck, his suspicions of the mystery woman were confirmed as he turned the corner and saw that the Jeep was gone.

See? Nothing to worry about. Now get a move on and find a good place to park before the sun sets. You can't go another night on only twenty minutes of sleep. Rest up and start early tomorrow.

Within moments, Dewight was back on the road and heading south again. Continuing his journey down Route 2, he soon reached the other end of Yelk. As he crossed over the town line, he glanced in his rearview mirror. What he saw reflecting back almost caused him to jump right out of his own skin.

Practically tailgating his truck was the same Jeep from Sal's Diner.

Without thinking, Dewight slammed on the gas and started to pick up speed. Eyes darting from the moving road to his rearview mirror, he hoped to leave the Jeep behind in a cloud of brown dust. But, as soon as he started to speed up, so did the Jeep.

"Fuck! Fuck!" Dewight yelled, pounding his fist on the steering wheel as he neared 80mph. He was so sure back at the diner that he was in the clear, one full step ahead of anyone that might be looking for him. But, somehow, they'd managed to find him. The woman in camouflage at the counter was undoubtably an undercover cop, probably sent in to observe Dewight before the official arrest was made. Any moment now, he suspected to see a fleet of cruisers, helicopters, and attack drones come streaming over the horizon in a cacophony of flashing blue lights and sirens. This realization of impending capture left Dewight with only two options.

He could either pull over and surrender, undoubtedly spending the rest of his natural life rotting in a prison cell.

Or, he could go out in a blaze of glory and hope that Janis would be there waiting for him on the other side.

Approaching a small intersection at the end of a long hill, Dewight flicked his blinker on and began to slow down. Seconds later, the Jeep did the same. Veering to the left, blinker still ticking, Dewight began to pull over. But just as he was about to take the turn, he cranked the truck to the right and floored the gas again. Tires squealing, kicking up loose pavement at the stalled Jeep as it skidded to a stop in the middle of the left-hand lane, Dewight's truck spun in a full circle; hot rubber peeling fresh lines across the square of cracked asphalt. When he finally screeched to a stop, he was facing the rear of the Jeep. Without hesitation, Dewight jumped out of the truck and raised his gun.

"Put your hands up or I'll shoot!" he screamed, leaning down behind the open door for cover. With both hands, he steadied the weapon as best her could. Slowly, the figure behind the wheel obeyed and raised both hands out the open window. "Open the door from the outside and step out!" Dewight was amazed at how quickly the roles had reversed themselves. Here he was, ready to shoot an undercover cop if they so much as flinched. He couldn't think about it too hard though and lose his nerve. One hand still raised out the window, the driver opened the door and stepped out.

Just as he suspected, it was the mystery woman from the diner. Heavy camouflage jacket and scraggly ponytail billowing in the gusts of passing wind, the bill of her trucker hat was pulled down low over her eyes.

Gun still leveled, Dewight stood up from his crouching position behind the truck door. "Lace your fingers behind your head and drop to your knees! Now!" Fat beads of sweat stung his eyes as both hands kept the barrel of the pistol trained on the woman. When she failed to drop to the ground, merely continuing to stand in the middle of the empty intersection like a lost scarecrow, Dewight yelled, "I'm not kidding! Get on the goddamn ground, or I'll—"

"We have to leave, Dewight!" the woman suddenly yelled, hands still raised above her head. "We don't have much time! They're coming!"

Dewight stepped fully out from behind the shield of the door and took one step forward. "Who are you?! How do you know my name?!"

"There's no time to explain!" the woman yelled, her head whipping back and forth at the empty hillside that surrounded them. Dewight hesitated to react, thoroughly baffled by what he was hearing. Sensing his reluctance, the woman took one brazen step forward. "Please! They are getting close! Hurry up and come with me if you want to stay free!"

With no time to weigh his options, Dewight lowered his gun. "Pull the Jeep up to my truck. I have a few bags to load in the back."

CHAPTER 10

"I have some updates on that hold up at the Ubit store in Kittery, sir," a trooper said as he walked into Sgt. Morrow's office in the State Police barracks. Sgt. Morrow, scrolling through his personal messages on his phone, looked up from behind his desk and motioned for the trooper to close the door behind him before continuing.

Once the door was latched shut, Morrow set his phone down on the top of his desk and leaned back slowly in his chair. "What you got for me?"

"As you already know, we talked to the store clerk and got his description of the man who held him at gunpoint. After that, we attempted to contact someone at Ubit headquarters to release the video footage from the surveillance cameras inside the store. Somebody in their security department finally got back to us and transferred the video." From his pocket, the trooper produced a video projection pod and held it up to the sergeant.

Intrigued, Morrow stood up from his desk and joined the trooper on the far side of the room. "Let's see it." Setting the small cylinder on the edge of the desk, both men stood back while the video file downloaded. Once complete, the cylinder emitted a three-dimensional picture on the space of blank wall on one side of the room. In full color and depth—as if the men were standing in the real store, only from a crow's nest position in the high left-hand corner of the room—the projection began to play.

It showed a man, clad in dirty denim jeans and a work shirt, walk casually into the store and begin looking around. It was apparent after the first couple seconds that the man wasn't looking around at the many gadgets that cluttered the aisles and walls. He was looking for someone in particular. Once he found the store clerk, they both walked over to the counter, which was directly under the eye of the camera. There, projected image facing the two officers, was the man they were looking for in clear view. It took Morrow all of two seconds to identify the stoic figure standing before him.

"Pause the footage," he said abruptly to the cylinder. Its voice activated functions heard the command and froze the frame. Slowly, arms folded behind the small of his back, Morrow approached the wall and got a closer look. "God damnit... I should've known," he said under his breath, eyes squinting at the vibrant, lifelike particles of the floating image.

"Sir?" the trooper asked, confused at Morrow's sudden reaction.

Without turning away from the still frame, Morrow said, "Did the clerk see the vehicle that the suspect was driving?"

The trooper paused for a moment to check his notes from a miniature tablet in his front pocket before saying, "No, he hid behind the counter after the perp left. But the cameras posted on the outside of the building did."

"And?"

"The suspect parked too far away from the store for his license plate to be analyzed. But I was able to get a make and model on the truck. It's some rusted out piece of shit Ford, an antique to say the least."

"A farm truck, perhaps?" Morrow asked as he broke away from the projection and sat back down behind his desk. This all but confirmed his suspicions of who the armed man was. The death of Janis Jones was still entirely too fresh in his mind. It had only been a little over twelve hours since he left Dewight Jones—angry and broken—on that starlit porch.

I knew we would be seeing each other again. But I was hoping it wouldn't be so soon, Morrow thought, wishing that this was just another typical robbery case. But, this was far from a robbery; this was an act of unbridled angst. Crimes of the heart were always risky business for everyone involved, including police. In Morrow's many years of experience, a man with nothing to lose was by far the worst kind of person to pursue.

"Possibly… sounds like you got someone in mind, sir."

Without answering the question, Morrow said, "I need you to go out to the Jones farm right away. The same one we took the body out of last night. I have a feeling that Dewight Jones won't be home, but in case he is, do not engage. Hold the man in question on the property and wait for back up. Do not put him into custody. I will arrive and interview the suspect myself."

A worried look came over the trooper's young, shaven face. "Back up? Sir, I don't really think that's necessary if I'm we aren't going to arrest—"

"Just do it!" Morrow bellowed, jumping up from his chair and leaning over the top of his desk. "Once you get there, be sure to call me whether he is there or not. Now, go. I have to make some phone calls."

Not wanting to feel the full wrath of Morrow's sudden anger, the trooper nodded in agreement and quickly left the office. As soon as the door latched shut again, Morrow let out a heavy sigh and rested his head in his hands.

I told him not to go chasing ghosts, Morrow thought. *Nothing good ever comes out of it. Violence begets violence... and there are no happy endings for those who travel that path in life.* But Morrow suspected that Dewight Jones already knew that. And, in all honesty, was exactly what scared Morrow the most. Morrow had developed an unusual empathy for Dewight Jones. The man had just gone through one of the worst things any man could endure. And given the same set of circumstances, Morrow might see himself following the same path of self-destruction. This ongoing situation needed to be handled with kid gloves; going in heavy and trying to make Dewight surrender would undoubtedly end in unnecessary bloodshed on both sides.

Suddenly, like a flower popping up through the dark soils of his memory, an old saying his grandfather used to say resurfaced to see the light.

"There ain't no rest for a man seeking justice for those that were unfairly taken from him before their time," he said to the empty walls of his office, his grandfather's voice ringing out between his ears. "The only peace of mind he will ever find is in his own demise."

CHAPTER 11

"There better be some progress to report," Dr. Smith said angrily to no one in particular as she crossed the floor of the research center at Ubit Industries Headquarters. "Those jackasses at the U.N. and the global media are blowing up all the phones in the building demanding an update."

There were currently one hundred employees working in revolving shifts around the clock in the research center. And, just as Dr. Smith had threatened, no one was allowed to leave the building until the crisis was solved for good. A row of dingy cots was set up in the back room by the toilet, all meals were brought in by trusted employees from other sectors who had clearance to enter the area. Anyone who did try to gain access or leave the high security area was met by the opposition of heavily armed men. Stationed on both sides of the Research Lab doors, they stood there like meat-made totem poles in dark sunglasses and clutched their semi-automatic weapons.

Since the initial press release, lots of members of the press had tried to gain entry to the lab with fake credentials and were met with nothing short of extreme resistance. The evolving news of S.A.M.A.N.T.H.A.'s potential malfunction was all that everyone around the world was talking about. The P.H.R.G. were responsible for most of the media gossip about system malfunctions being the real cause of the rising user deaths, only adding to the mystique of the story. Despite constant meddling from outside forces, Ubit had still managed to keep everything under wraps so far. But, sooner or later, someone would slip through the cracks and find out what was really going on inside Dr. Smith's impenetrable fortress. It was inevitable. Nothing ever stayed a secret very long in these times of constant public surveillance and company whistle blowing. The damning truth was bound to come out unless Dr. Smith and her team could get S.A.M.A.N.T.H.A. back under control. And fast.

"We are making strides, Dr. Smith," Professor Yamura—now acting head of the Ubit Developmental Research team—said, turning away from the twenty-foot high-def monitor that was anchored in the center of the vast room. The giant screen showed an overlay of the ongoing progress of each individual researcher as they all simultaneously attempted to re-code S.A.M.A.N.T.H.A.'s programming. Cultured in the ways of the far West, he bowed solemnly to Dr. Smith in a sign of respect as she approached.

"Stand up straight," Dr. Smith said curtly, wasting no time on acknowledging his foreign social etiquette. "Now, fill me in on what's going on. Pronto."

Yamura complied immediately and stiffened back up to a straight standing position. Waiving one smooth hand over at the monitor, he said, "As you can see, we have every single man and woman on the floor stripping apart S.A.M.A.N.T.H.A.'s genetic code bank from every angle. Little by little, we are reaching the root of the problem."

Dr. Smith nodded, cold eyes sweeping over the jumble of projected numbers and stats. Turning back swiftly to Yamura, she asked, "And what about the user fatalities? Have they plateaued yet?"

For the first time since meeting, Yamura's face showed a clear sign of human emotion. Brows creased and mouth slanted downward, he sighed deeply then said, "Well... I wouldn't exactly say... I mean... we are all working very hard. But without shutting off the program from global use while—"

Without warning, Dr. Smith grabbed the small statured man by the lapels of his white lab coat and jerked him up off the ground. Pressing his back against the screen, face pushed into his, she grunted, "Don't give me that horseshit. Are user deaths subsiding? Yes or no?"

"... no," Yamura eventually whispered, his thin lips trembling ever so slightly with fear. He'd heard briefly about Dr. Smith from fellow colleagues before taking the red eye flight from Japan to America, how she was very passionate about her work, almost to a fault. But now, suspended in the air by the front of his shirt like a bullied child, he saw that the word passionate had been used as nothing more than a polite term for her tyrannical oversight.

Slowly, Dr. Smith lowered Yamura back to his feet and smoothed the wrinkles out of his jacket. "I see... do I dare ask what the current mortality rate is?"

Yamura knew he was staring down the barrel of a loaded question. If he answered honestly, he risked more physical and verbal assault. But, if he didn't answer at all— or worse, lie—his fate might be much worse. Running his fingers nervously through the short length of his jet-black hair, Yamura hesitated for a moment before mumbling, "As of approximately 8:00 this morning... just over five thousand worldwide, ma'am." As soon as the words left his lips, he braced himself for the worst, clenching his eyes shut and tensing every muscle in his body while waiting for impact.

But that didn't happen.

Surprisingly, Dr. Smith didn't strike him down or scream in his face. Instead, she let out a great bellow of laughter as she looked about the crowded room. "Great! You hear that, everyone?!" She twirled around to the surrounding fleet of scientists that sat in their cramped cubicles, pretending not to eavesdrop on the conversation. One by one, they sheepishly poked their heads up over the top of their monitors to watch Dr. Smith. "Because of your imbecilic laziness, over five thousand users are now dead... five thousand!" Slowly, she scanned the circumference of the room as she spoke. "Of course, the loss of these poor, innocent souls weighs no significance on me... oh, no. The blame for this tragedy is placed squarely on all of YOU!" Her judgmental finger swept across the hundreds of tired eyes that glared back at her. "You know what that means? Hm? It means that the longer you pathetic dweebs sit here and twiddle your thumbs, the more innocent users will drop dead! And what good is a dead user to a tech company?! Your collective ignorance is flushing trillions and trillions of dollars down the goddamn drain!"

The doctors hate filled words floated heavily in the silence of the room. Her voice, harsh and guttural like a mountain lion, caused several scientists to urinate in their pants. Not one of them dared to point out that it was Dr. Smith who demanded that the program remain open while the rewrites were being made, making the task nearly impossible to complete in any timely manner. This lack of empathy on her part ensured more senseless fatalities, making the whole scenario feel like a pointless death march for everyone involved behind the scenes.

Everyone, except Dr. Kara Smith.

Seeing that her point was made, Dr. Smith turned back to Yamura and quietly said, "Fix this now, or I'll be shipping you back to Japan in a cardboard box. Got it?"

Beyond frightened, Yamura did a quick bow and spun away so he wouldn't have to face the heat from Dr. Smith's hardboiled stare. He saw evil in those eyes, a dark passenger that knew no human boundaries of the soul.

When her eyes left Yamura to scrutinize the individual stations around the room, everyone quickly ducked behind the safety of their monitors and began vigorously typing. Satisfied, Dr. Smith made the long walk back to the only exit in the lab. But, as she ordered the guards to step aside and unlock the door so she could get through, they instead stood their ground and looked worryingly at each other over the rims of their dark glasses.

"What is it?" Dr. Smith demanded, the toe of her stiletto tapping impatiently on the hard-tiled floor. "I don't have time for secret handshakes, boys. So, step aside and let—"

The large man with the face tattoo stationed on the left roughly cleared his throat and said in a baritone voice, "Ma'am… we can't let you through right now. There appears to be a security issue on the other side."

Shocked, Dr. Smith placed her hands impatiently on her hips. "Security issue? Of what sort?"

Pressing one finger to his wireless earpiece, the guard listened for a moment to the tiny voice in his ear then nodded. "There's a government agent trying to gain access to the research facility. He has two armed men with him—"

But as the guard was speaking, Dr. Smith shoved her way past the two men and out the door. Just as the guard had said, as the steel reinforced door swung open, she found herself face to face with three men in dark suits. Each one had a laminated government issued badge pinned to the front of their jackets, their eyes momentarily lighting up with surprise when Dr. Smith appeared from the other side of the door. Along with those badges, the butts of their holstered service weapons were clearly visible.

"Hello, gentlemen," she said, stepping confidently towards them. Making sure to keep a good distance, Dr. Smith put on a friendly face and asked, "What can I help you with today?"

Snapping out of his trance like state, the leader of the small group stepped forward and said, "I'm agent Clemens with the F.B.I., Ms. Smith. I have a warrant for your arrest."

"Please, call me Dr. Smith," she said, smiling affectionately. "May I ask what this warrant is in reference to?"

"You are currently being investigated for the unexplained deaths of thousands of your program users, in addition to the destruction of a government issued android that was sent here yesterday." The man dipped a hand into the inside pocket of his coat and produced a paper form that listed all the offenses that Dr. Smith was being accused of. The list was long; everything from unlawful use of private data, destruction of government property, and crimes against humanity were on the dossier. As if reaching his hand out to a live rattle snake, Clemens held the letter out cautiously towards Dr. Smith so she could review its contents.

Without skipping a beat, Dr. Smith brushed the letter aside and asked, "And what if I refuse to go with you? What then? As you can see, I have a lot of work to do here and am possibly the only person who can stop these... unfortunate mishaps."

Shoving the paper back into his coat pocket, Clemens glanced back at the two armed men standing at his side and nodded. In one motion, they drew the handguns from their side holsters and approached Dr. Smith. As both men reached out to grip her arms, Dr. Smith's guards lunged forward at lightning speed. With brute strength, the extended arms of the two F.B.I. agents were suddenly bent sideways, elbows loudly snapping at an irregular angle. Screaming out in pain, both agents attempted to bring around their pistols with their good arms and shoot their attackers. In unison, both guards kicked the pistols from the agent's hands and slammed them face first to the floor.

"Well, what to do now, agent Clemens?" Dr. Smith asked, stepping lightly over the two crippled agents and closing the gap between her and Clemens. Face to face, she languished in the expression of pure terror that was melted across his painfully ordinary face. Right hand drifting to the gun at his hip, Clemens was about to try and reassert his authority when six more guards came rushing in from down the hall. Standing tall behind Dr. Smith, a row of dedicated soldiers ready to defend their fearless leader surrounded Clemens like a mountain of muscle.

Seeing his naked fear crippling any other action other than dumbfounded silence, Dr. Smith smiled. "Here are your choices, agent. You can either end up on the floor, crying and broken like your friends here." She gestured briefly to the squirming agents that were still pinned under the heavy boots of her lackies. "Or, you can walk out of here in one piece—all appendages still intact—and go back to your political cronies with a message."

Mouth impossibly dry, Clemens forced moisture to his lips before numbly saying, "And what message would that be?"

"That Ubit Industries answers to no one," Dr. Smith said taciturnly, condescending smile faded to a wicked scowl. "If the government wants answers, they can wait in line with the rest of the world."

Outnumbered and out gunned, Clemens nodded somberly in agreement.

That twisted smile seeped back onto Dr. Smith's face as she snapped her fingers. Like trained monkeys, the guards backed away and allowed the agents to scramble up off the floor. Holding their broken limbs, tears staining the fronts of their dark suits, they weakly gathered their guns from the corner of the room and headed for the door. But just as Clemens and his damaged backup were about to exit through the front lobby, he turned back to Dr. Smith and said, "We both know that this doesn't end here. The government will get what they want, one way or another."

Smile beaming, bleached teeth sharp and eyes full of flame, Dr. Smith crossed her arms. "The next time your bosses send someone in here to try and take me down, they better be ready for war."

This time, it was Clemens who had a wide smile; his last retort drifting across the room like napalm fumes caught in a thin breeze. "Oh, they will, Dr. Smith. Just you wait and see."

CHAPTER 12

After ditching his truck in the middle of the deserted intersection on the outskirts of Yelk, Dewight jumped into the passenger seat of the mystery woman's Jeep. They sped onward into the mountainside, putting much needed distance between Dewight and the authorities that were undoubtably chasing after him. But, Dewight couldn't be completely sure of his driver's true intentions. Not able to find it in himself to fully trust his new traveling partner, he rested the loaded pistol on his lap as they barreled towards the dwindling sunset on the horizon.

"Tell me who you are," Dewight demanded as they got deeper and deeper into the countryside, his tone flat and void of empathy. A part of him wanted to trust this woman, but his strong sense of cynicism knew better than to believe anything a stranger had to say. For all he knew, she was playing him for a fool; telling him exactly what he wanted to hear as a means of disarming him until they were somewhere more secure. Then, she would turn him over to the cops, possibly to collect a reward or bounty that might be on his head.

"My name is Lisa," the woman said, her bright eyes never leaving the ever-darkening road. "And I'd appreciate if you didn't point that thing at me. It's distracting." One hand on the wheel, Lisa removed the floppy trucker cap from her head. She tossed it over her shoulder into the back seat with Dewight's bags, exposing a thick growth of vibrant chestnut colored hair underneath. The loose ponytail she had before was completely gone, allowing her curls to spring freely around her shoulders. In the crisp, orange rays of dwindling sunlight, Dewight couldn't help but admire her smooth skin, button nose, and elegant eyebrows as she continued to center her concentration on the road ahead.

Forcing himself to ignore her obvious beauty, seeing it only as further evidence that he was sitting in the middle of a trap, Dewight gripped his fingers a little tighter around the pistol as he replied, "Not 'till you tell me how you know who I am. And why you want to help me so badly."

"Like you, Dewight, I am a fellow Purist." The statement was left to sink in, filling the empty space of the cab as the never-ending line of towering trees whizzed by. Once she was sure Dewight wasn't going to automatically reject the idea, Lisa continued, "My friends and I saw your little show at the Ubit store in Kittery. We want to help you on your mission."

Brain clouded, Dewight stammered, "I... what? How could you possibly know I'm a Purist?" He thought for a moment before adding, "Even more so, how do you know about what I did in Kittery? That only happened this morning."

"I'm part of a group of... consciences objectors, if you will," Lisa said casually, as if she had recited these words many times before. "By any means necessary, we oppose the gradual overhaul of the human race that advances in modern technology is solely responsible for. We call ourselves the P.H.R.G.—the Purists Human Rights Group."

"The P.H.R.G.? Am I supposed to know what that is?"

Lisa laughed, her smooth lips parting to expose neat rows of shiny white teeth. "I suspected that you wouldn't. We get some publicity, mainly by spreading the truth about Ubit, but are relatively unknown to the public. Ubit has the money and resources to bury most of the dirt we send along to the media. Most... but not all."

"That doesn't explain how you know who I am," Dewight said coldly, still not seeing the point of Lisa's rambling. He felt as if he was being recruited into a cult, one that forced its followers to abduct strangers and bore them into submission with anti-technological rhetoric.

Even from behind the wheel, Lisa could feel Dewight's resistance. So, she got right to the facts. "We have a somebody on the inside at Ubit Industries. As soon as your little stunt in Kittery got back to corporate, a copy of the video footage was secretly forwarded to our headquarters. After analyzing the footage, I was sent out by my superiors to find you."

"Find me? What the hell for?"

"To help see your mission through. We heard everything you said in that store, about the factory in Portland and how S.A.M.A.N.T.H.A. ruined your life. We want to help you take it down. Not just for us, Dewight, but for every single soul that Ubit is systematically destroying with their corrupted technology." Bravely, Lisa's right hand drifted from the steering wheel and rested gently on Dewight's left knee. "We need to avenge those lost souls, Dewight. We need to avenge Janis."

Hearing his late wife's name felt bitter-sweet to his ears. Now torn in two by grief, Dewight's paranoia told him he shouldn't trust some phantom organization he'd never heard of. But his common sense played a totally different tune in his head.

Whether you like it or not, you can't carry out this plan of yours alone. You're going up against the biggest corporation to ever exist. EVER. And to make things worse, they know you're coming now. If this little ragtag group of activists know your plan, then so does Ubit. They'll be expecting you now, be sure of that. No doubt armed to the teeth. But, if you team up with others who share the same moralistic drive to set things right, then you might actually stand a chance. I know you went into this out of grief driven anger—just looking to lash out at the system—but perhaps now you can do more than just take down one measly factory. Maybe... just maybe... you can shut down the whole damn system. Someone's gotta do it. Why not you?

It seemed impossible for one person, even backed by a group, to obtain such a revolutionary feat, but what did he have to lose now? His initial thoughts of revenge never made it past the dismantling of a single factory, an extreme oversight he was only now considering. Dewight had secretly assumed he'd die trying to carry out his crazy plan. But now, cruising along backwoods trails with someone who he didn't quite trust, Dewight was finally thinking ahead. For better or worse, he needed help. And this meeting of chance was probably his only lifeline left.

"Alright. I'm in." Receiving the answer she so desperately needed to hear, Lisa's hand left Dewight's knee and wrapped itself back around the steering wheel.

Now full dusk—the sweeping night sky twinkling with hidden constellations untouched by the poison light of the city—the Jeep's headlights were the only thing illuminating the dark soils of the winding dirt trail. As the road gradually got bumpier and more secluded, Dewight turned to Lisa and asked, "Where are we going?"

"To the P.H.R.G. hide out," she said. "There's a couple people you need to meet before we start. We still have a bit of a drive, so sit back and get some rest."

With nothing left to say, Dewight re-holstered his pistol into the front pocket of his jeans and leaned back. Head resting against the soft cushion of the seat, his eyes began to succumb to the lull of the engine as it pushed them along into the night. Feeling his eyes begin to grow heavy with the sands of sleep, a single thought drifted from Dewight's still conscious mind.

I'm coming to see you Janis. One way or another... we will be together again soon, my love.

Her pleasant smile and crystal dotted eyes were the last thing he saw with his mind's eye before succumbing to the inevitable pulls of much need slumber.

***

At the same time that Dewight was drifting to sleep in the passenger seat of Lisa's Jeep, Sgt. Morrow was racing to a dispatch call on the outskirts of Yelk. He had been busy rummaging for clues at the Jones family farm for several hours when a call came in over the radio that an officer had located Dewight's truck in the next town over. Making no progress in his search of the deserted home, Morrow dropped what he was doing and jumped in his cruiser.

On his way to the scene, he was informed over the radio that the suspect was still nowhere to be found, but Morrow would bet dollars to donuts that there was at least something left behind in the truck that would help point them in the right direction. Blue lights on and sirens blaring, he pushed the needle through Kittery into Yelk. When he finally got to the taped off intersection, he saw a swarm of uniformed officers and forensics crews already hard at work. Wasting no time, Morrow threw his squad car into park at the mouth of the scene and crossed the yellow tape.

"What we got? Anything good?" Morrow said to a trooper as he approached the truck. The trooper was sitting in the driver's seat, scanning for prints on the steering wheel, when Morrow ducked his head into the open door and visually inspected the interior. Against what he was initially expecting, he didn't see any obvious signs of a struggle—no blood stains, broken glass, or bullet holes. For all intents and purposes, it appeared to be just another abandoned vehicle with nothing out of the ordinary inside. This absence of evidence only further confused Morrow.

Turning away from the handheld scanner, the trooper joined Morrow outside of the truck so another forensics person could gain access and collect fibers from the seats. "Not much, sir. We can confirm that it's Dewight Jones truck, but we have no idea where he took off to."

Perplexed, Morrow rubbed at the cleft of his chin as he thought. "Has anyone in the area called in anything fishy tonight? Car jackings? Attempted break-ins"

"No, sir. We even had drones search the entire two-mile radius of the surrounding area in case he was hiding out in the woods somewhere nearby, but found nothing. He's just vanished."

"This makes no sense," Morrow grumbled, taking a slow walk around the exterior of the truck. Besides being incredibly out of date, the old pickup looked to be in working condition. There was no oil or gas leaking from the bottom, no dents or dings in its body. Even the tires were well balanced and full of air. As he made his way back around to the driver's side, Morrow peeked back into the cab and checked the gas gauge. It showed that there was well over half a tank of gas sitting in the tank.

Strange. Why would he ditch his truck like this? Morrow pondered, struggling to see the whole picture. *I'm sure he knew we would be coming after him, no doubt of that. But still... he had a hell of a head start ahead of us. Surely, he didn't think he'd be better off on foot. Did he? No, that's crazy. I met that man and, even in his love-torn state, he didn't strike me as stupid. There has to be more to this that I'm not seeing.*

Leaning back out of the truck, Morrow turned to the trooper at his side. "Did you find anything in the truck that could be of use?"

From his back pocket, the trooper produced a small plastic bag and promptly handed it to Morrow. Holding the bag up to the mounted floodlights posted over the intersection, he stared longingly at the small piece of paper that sat in the middle of the plastic belly.

"A receipt?"

"Found it on the passenger seat," the trooper said, swatting away a few fat mosquitoes who were trying to get a free meal under the glare of the powerful halogen lights. "It's from a small diner a few miles back called Sal's Place. I sent an officer up there to question the staff, turns out our guy went in there earlier today and got some grub. Entered the diner and left the diner alone. The waitress working positively identified him from a freeze frame from the Ubit store surveillance video."

Handing the receipt back to the trooper, Morrow asked, "Did she say anything else? Was he acting strange? Happen to say where he was going?"

"No such luck," the trooper shrugged. "She said he ordered his food, paid, and left. No chitchat. Seemed like just another local type, nothing out of the ordinary. The only peculiar thing she remembered about him was that he asked a lot of questions about the food. Whether it was fresh and whatnot. Kind of weird, I guess."

Morrow couldn't help but snicker to himself upon hearing that. *Of course*, he thought, *you're out in the real world now, aren't ya? No more of that farm raised beef and fresh vegetables. Not for you.* Morrow secretly took joy in the fact that at least Dewight was uncomfortable in this little game of cat and mouse. If Dewight was smart, and Morrow was betting that he was, he'd adapt quickly. But Morrow had a sneaking suspicion that this old farm boy would have a bit of a hard time adjusting to the fast-moving ways of the world. Morrow could only hope that this fundamental flaw might be the thread to Dewight's own undoing.

Poking back out from inside his head, Morrow cleared his throat and asked, "So, all you found was this receipt? Nothing else?"

"No, sir," the trooper said, an expression of slight disappointment flashing across his tragically plain face. "We're lifting prints from the interior now to see if maybe he had an accomplice. I was thinking that perhaps someone picked him up at this intersection, and they drove off in a different vehicle together. A sort of prearranged meeting spot."

Morrow didn't think this was likely, given Dewight's deeply ingrained loner personality. He didn't strike Morrow as the kind of man who asked for help from anyone, let alone with avenging the death of his beloved wife. But, at this point, he was ready to consider anything that might bring him closer to finding his man before something terrible happened. And, given Dewight's increasing impulsiveness, something was bound to happen unless Morrow could get to him in time to foil his plan.

Suddenly, Morrow got an idea on a possible lead. It was a stretch, but if he pulled the right strings, he might be able to at least find out if Dewight had found himself a partner or not.

"I have a feeling you're not going to find anyone else's prints in there," Morrow said over his shoulder as he began his determined stride back to the cruiser, "but if you do, be sure to call me right away. Same goes for anything else of interest that you might find in there."

The trooper nodded as he watched Morrow duck back under the barrier of yellow tape. "Can do, sir. It's going to be a late night here." Curiously, knowing Morrow was following some kind of intuition that all veteran cops seemed to possess, he called out from the edge of the tape. "Say... you got something you want to tell me?"

Before climbing in behind the wheel of his cruiser, Morrow turned back towards the trooper and said, "I have a hunch. Might be nothing... but it's worth checking out anyway. I'll keep you posted." The trooper attempted to prod further, but Morrow was already revving the engine of his squad car and peeling away back towards the barracks.

On the tail end of a fourteen-hour shift, driving along with nothing to keep him company but the guiding light of the full moon, a funny thought occurred to Morrow.

Now you got me chasing after ghosts, friend. The only difference is that, come hell or high water, I'm gonna get what I'm after. And when I do, I'll live to tell the story.

***

Unable to sleep, Dr. Smith found herself staring at the same naked moon that guided Sgt. Morrow on his way back to the State Trooper barracks. Sitting alone in her office—lights dimmed and doors locked shut—she idly held a glass of expensive gin as her eyes searched the night sky for any answers that the archaic heavens might be hiding. Unable to leave Ubit Industry Headquarters, in fear of the authorities ambushing her as soon as she stepped out into the street, Dr. Smith knew she was playing a very dangerous game now. Her brash move to not comply with the powers that be could not only dismantle her entire life's work, but also cost her everything. Her freedom, her pride, her life were all on the line. And the line was getting thinner all the time.

They want to lock me up, and for what? she thought bitterly, sipping at the tumbler of aged gin that she clasped absentmindedly in one hand. *Simple minded fools. They can't begin to grasp the importance of my work, choosing to instead focus on the minor screw ups. If it was up to people like them, mankind would still be shitting in outhouses and pulling out unwanted pregnancies with rusty clothes hangers in back alleyways. It's a fact that all great advancements in human history came with some negative side effects. This doesn't mean that the progressive technology in question is bad, no no. This is merely a formality, an offshoot. As the old saying goes, "You gotta break a few eggs if you wanna make an omelet."*

Dr. Smith sincerely believed this notion, more than anything else in her life right now. So what if half the world had to die? That was the price of progress. Some could say that they lived more through their time spent with S.A.M.A.N.T.H.A. then they ever could have in a million lifetimes. What Dr. Smith had provided the world was invaluable beyond comprehension. She could see that so clearly, so why couldn't the pesky heads of world government trying to shut down her whole operation see it? They didn't know what it was like to obtain this level of greatness and were probably jealous of the fact. All those number crunching bureaucrats and phony politicians knew was dirty money and dishonesty. For too long they used the ignorance of the common citizen to lift themselves up to heights of unfathomable power. But now that there was something bigger than them, mightier and more influential than all their efforts combined, they felt threatened.

And why wouldn't they? I made them virtually obsolete. No one is a slave to their rule when using S.A.M.A.N.T.H.A. The power of all life choices lies squarely on the user, the way every true existence was meant to be. Turning her attention away from the sky, Dr. Smith spun in her chair. Setting her gin down to the side, she picked up a single manila folder that lay inconspicuously in the center of her desk. Printed in bold red ink on the front were the letters P.H.R.G. Thumbing through the dense file for maybe the hundredth time that night, Dr. Smith looked over her long-time efforts and smiled.

What those idiots in Washington don't know is that I've been planning for this all along. I knew when I made S.A.M.A.N.T.H.A. that there was a possibility of her becoming sentient. Just as I foresaw this worst-case scenario, I also knew that someday my power would be resented by those who longed for my reach. Even now, with thousands of users across the world dying around the clock, I'm still one step ahead.

The folder contained top secret information about the P.H.R.G. and all its known members. All of which was obtained by a double agent working secretly for Ubit Industries. This agent, which only Dr, Smith had direct contact with, worked right in the heart of the P.H.R.G. and reported back to her weekly with any vital information. For years, Dr. Smith allowed the group to leak certain things to the media to keep up appearances, all the while playing a fool and biding her time to strike.

"In due time, I'll flip the tables on those slimy cavemen," Dr. Smith said excitedly to herself, the empty walls of her office draped in darkness. "They think they're going to take me down, take down Ubit Industries and S.A.M.A.N.T.H.A., and I'll let them think that. For a little while longer, anyway." Slowly, she picked back up her tumbler of gin and rose from her chair. Standing at the window, looking out at the oozing light of the city skyline, she sipped longingly at the dry liquid. With a wicked smile dripped across her face, Dr. Smith tilted her head back and laughed to the flat face of the hanging moon.

"They think they're going to save the world. But the only thing they'll be saving is my legacy. S.A.M.A.N.T.H.A. is mine; always has been and always will be. The deaths will stop when I say so. You'll see… they'll all see."